NL

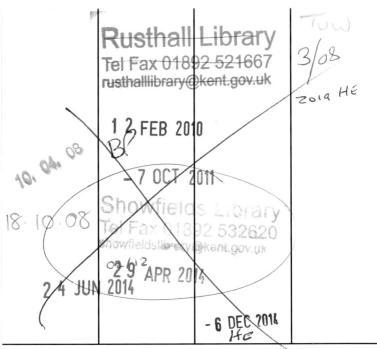
Please return on or before the latest date above.
You can renew online at *www.kent.gov.uk/libs*
or by telephone 08458 247 200

CUSTOMER SERVICE EXCELLENCE **Libraries & Archives**

Kent
County
Council

GUNSMOKE OVER TEXAS

GUNSMOKE OVER TEXAS

BRADFORD SCOTT

WHEELER
CHIVERS

This Large Print edition is published by Wheeler Publishing, Waterville, Maine, USA and by BBC Audiobooks Ltd, Bath, England.
Wheeler Publishing is an imprint of The Gale Group.
Wheeler is a trademark and used herein under license.

The text of this Large Print edition is unabridged.
Other aspects of the book may vary from the original edition.
Set in 16 pt. Plantin.

LIBRARY OF CONGRESS CATALOGING-IN-PUBLICATION DATA

Scott, Bradford, 1893–1975.
  Gunsmoke over Texas : a Walt Slade western / by Bradford Scott.
    p. cm. — (Wheeler Publishing large print western)
  ISBN-13: 978-1-59722-640-0 (pbk. : lg. print : alk. paper)
  ISBN-10: 1-59722-640-8 (pbk. : lg. print : alk. paper)
  I. Title.
PS3537.C9265G86 2007
813'.52—dc22   2007029056

BRITISH LIBRARY CATALOGUING-IN-PUBLICATION DATA AVAILABLE

Published in 2007 in the U.S. by arrangement with
Golden West Literary Agency.
Published in 2008 in the U.K. by arrangement with
Golden West Literary Agency.

U.K. Hardcover: 978 1 405 64304 7 (Chivers Large Print)
U.K. Softcover: 978 1 405 64305 4 (Camden Large Print)

Printed in the United States of America on permanent paper
10 9 8 7 6 5 4 3 2 1

GUNSMOKE OVER TEXAS

ONE

From where Ranger Walt Slade sat his great black horse on the rimrock trail, the oil-strike town of Weirton looked like a cluster of fallen stars spread haphazard over the prairie. The smoke cloud that hung over the town reflected the glow luridly and in the bright moonlight the forest of derricks was clearly visible as a spiderweb tracery of shadows under the pall of smoke.

To the west of Weirton, with the rimrock trail running along their crest, was a range of jagged hills marching into the north as far as the eye could see. To the north and to the east were more hills, misty with distance, mere purple shadows against the star-strewn blue-black of the Texas sky. Between the hills rolled the rangeland, grass grown prairie with streams flashing like silver snakes in the moonlight.

To the south the vista was different. Looking south, Slade seemed to be gazing over the edge of the world. About five miles from where Weirton sprawled beneath its smoke cloud the cap rock abruptly ended. The timbered and grass grown tableland gave way to a steep slope of rubble and debris that tumbled downward to the beginning of a stark desert hundreds of feet below. On this dead expanse the moonlight glittered weirdly and reflected back, just as during the day the rays of the sun would reflect back in scorching heat from the gleaming sands. No shade relieved the rock-strewn wasteland. The only vegetation was sparse sage, cactus in a thousand varieties and the ghostly, snake-like arms of the octillo. Miles distant flowed the Rio Grande with the old Chihuahua Trail, one of the freight routes into Mexico, crossing the uncertain waters via a rocky ford.

Slade's gaze came back from the stark desolation of the desert to the sultry glow of Weirton far below and some three miles east from the base of the hills.

"Well, Shadow, there it is," he told the horse. "The hell-kettle that's boiling over what used to be a peaceful cattle country. Looks like an interesting pueblo, even from here, and we've been hearing things about it all the way over from the post. Reckon Captain McNelty wasn't far wrong when he said it was the Devil's leavings dumped in God's front yard. Guess we might as well amble on down there and see what we can see. Understand this snake track drops down from the rim a few miles farther on and joins with the Chihuahua Trail, and that runs right past the town."

He gathered up the reins and sent Shadow ambling along the rimrock.

It was a pity that only Shadow was there to see the striking picture made by his master, named by the *peons* of the Rio Grande river villages El Halcon — the Hawk. Very tall, much more than six feet, the girth of his chest and the breadth of his shoulders matched his height. The white, still flood of the moonlight outlined his deeply bronzed face with its lean, powerful jaw and chin and strongly-curved nose and reflected from his gay, reckless gray eyes.

Under the broad brim of his pushed-back "J.B." his thick hair showed so black that a blue shadow seemed to lie upon it. With careless grace he wore the homely garb of the rangeland — faded overalls and soft blue shirt with a vivid neckerchief looped at the throat, batwing chaps and scuffed high-heeled half-boots of softly tanned leather. Double cartridge belts encircled his sinewy waist and from the carefully worked and oiled cut-out holsters protruded the plain black butts of heavy guns, from which his slender hands never seemed far away.

Suddenly Slade straightened in his saddle, his easy lounge changing to an attitude of attention. From the south and at no great distance had sounded a stutter of shots, a quick volley followed by silence. Now what in blazes! he wondered. Who'd be throwing lead up here, and why?

He leaned forward, listening intently for a repetition of the gunfire, which did not come. Then abruptly his grip tightened on the reins. Beating swiftly toward him from the south was a drumming of fast hoofs.

Slade glanced about. On the far side of the trail tall brush grew thickly. He spoke to Shadow and sent him ambling across the trail into the brush, regardless of thorns and raking branches. Men coming fast from the scene of a shooting might be in a nervous mood and a bit quick on the trigger. Better for him to see the approaching horsemen before they saw him.

Of course it might be just a bunch of sky-larking cowboys coming from town and shooting holes in the air. But Slade didn't think so. That abrupt volley had an ominous purposefulness to it unlike the firecracker banging of celebrating punchers.

Nearer came the speeding hoofs. Another moment and a fast riding troop flitted past Slade's place of concealment. He counted nine shadowy horsemen strung out along the trail. The last was bare of head and swayed in his saddle, leaning far over and gripping the pommel with one hand. To Slade, he looked very much like a gent who had recently leaned against the hot end of a passing bullet.

The riders vanished into the north. Slade sat listening till the hoofbeats were but a whisper before riding back to the trail. For a moment he hesitated, gazing after the invisible horsemen. Then he turned Shadow's head south. He had a hunch something had happened back there on the trail, something that could stand a little investigation.

Before he had covered half a mile his hunch proved to be a straight one. Lying in the trail was a huddled form. Nearby stood a saddled and bridled horse that snorted nervously as he drew near. Slade pulled Shadow to a halt; his eyes swept the trail, the growth. He listened intently for a moment, then dismounted quickly as the man on the ground moved a little and groaned. Slade knelt beside him and gently turned him over on his back. The moonlight fell full upon his face and Slade saw that he was little more than a boy, a slender young fellow, delicately featured, with a mop of curly brown hair; he wore rangeland garb.

Slade's black brows drew together as his glance fell on the dark stain spreading over the man's shirt just above the heart. With deft fingers he opened the shirt and shook his head at the sight of the small blue hole in the left breast from which oozed a few drops of blood. There was blood on the wounded man's lips, a bright froth, with a few bubbles coming and going as he breathed in stertorous gasps. He was hard hit, mighty hard hit. Slade's hands gently explored his back and felt a sticky dampness and a ragged tear in the cloth of the shirt; the bullet had gone clear through, and that bright froth on his lips meant internal arterial bleeding. Suddenly the young man's eyelids fluttered open. He stared dazedly at Slade.

"Take it easy," the ranger cautioned. "In much pain?"

"Not much," the other gasped reply, "except something seems sort of prodding inside; feels like it's poking my heart."

Slade cautiously examined the vicinity of the wound and his face was grave. There was undoubtedly a badly shattered rib; he could feel one broken end shoved up against the flesh. He greatly feared that the other splintered end was touching either the man's lung or his heart, probably the latter. The man needed a doctor in a hurry if he was to live. Meanwhile he'd do what he could and hope for the best.

"I'm going to strap you up as well as I can," he told the man. "Then I'll pack you to town or somewhere where you can get help. Don't try to tell me what happened now, just lie still and breathe as easy as you can."

Slade had a roll of bandage in his saddle pouch. He procured it and was turning back to the wounded man when his eye fell on something dark lying in the trail. He stooped and picked it up. It proved to be a greasy leather cap that showed much wear. On one side was a jagged tear.

The wounded man's broad-brimmed hat and his gun lay beside him. The cap must have belonged to the bare-headed horseman who had appeared to have been shot. Quite likely the wounded man had creased him with a slug before he went down. Slade thrust the cap into his saddle pouch and turned back to the wounded man. Working swiftly he bandaged his chest, covering the wounds in back and breast and drawing the cloth as tight as he thought advisable.

"Where you from, son?" he asked.

"Walking M ranch," the other whispered. "*Casa* is just about three miles north of where this trail hits the Chihuahua. Take me there. Can't miss it. Plain sight of trail. Tom Mawson's my dad. I'm Clate."

He spoke the name as if anybody should instantly know who Tom Mawson was. Doubtless a big ranchowner of the section, Slade decided.

"All right, Clate," he said. "No more talk now."

He lifted the boy's slight form in his arms, glanced at the roan horse still standing nearby and shook his head.

"Have to carry you in my arms," he told Clate. "Your cayuse can follow. Can't take a chance on any jolting."

Despite the burden of the wounded man he mounted Shadow easily, gathered up the reins and sent the big black north at a smooth running walk that covered ground fast but reduced jarring to a minimum. He was glad to note that Clate's eyes had closed again and that he lay motionless. Evidently he was unconscious, but his breathing remained the same.

The lights of the boom town on the prairie below fell behind, dwindled to pin points and finally winked out behind a bend. Another two miles and the trail dropped over the rimrock and wound and twisted down a dizzy slope. Half an hour later Shadow's irons rang on the hard surface of the Chihuahua.

The wounded man stirred in Slade's arms, groaned and opened his eyes. Slade noticed uneasily that his livid face was developing an ominous flush discernible even in the moonlight; he breathed with more difficulty.

"That dang sticking and prodding is getting worse," he gasped hoarsely. "I feel like I was going to blow up inside."

"Take it easy," Slade warned. "How much farther to go? We're on the Chihuahua now."

"Ranchhouse is right around the second bend," panted the other. "Maybe I'll get easier when I can lie down and straighten out."

"Sure to," Slade comforted him. "We'll soon have you fixed up okay."

Clate's eyes closed again but his breathing seemed even heavier, the flush staining his features more pronounced. Slade gazed anxiously ahead. He was pretty well convinced that if the wounded man didn't get attention soon he didn't have long to live.

Twenty minutes more and Slade breathed with relief as he sighted a fine big building

15

set in a grove of oaks, which he reasoned must be the Walking M ranchhouse. He turned Shadow into the yard, pulled up and shouted loudly.

Very quickly a light showed inside the building. The front door opened and a voice called, "What's the matter? Come on in."

Slade dismounted and strode up the veranda steps. A big old man with a shock of iron-gray hair peered toward him with outstretched neck.

"What in blazes —" he began.

"Man's hurt," Slade interrupted. "Says he lives here. You happen to be Tom Mawson?"

"That's right," the old man replied. "Bring him in. Who is — good God! My son!"

Two

"Steady," Slade cautioned. "Let me lay him down on something and then send for a doctor pronto. Where's the nearest one?"

"At Proctor, nearly ten miles to the north," answered Mawson. "Here, lay him on this couch."

As Slade crossed the room with his unconscious burden, Mawson rushed to the door and began roaring names. Alarmed shouts answered. Another minute and a dozen cowhands in all stages of undress came boil-

16

ing up the steps. Several carried guns. They glared suspiciously at Slade and began gabbling questions, but El Halcon's great voice abruptly cut through the uproar.

"Stop it!" he ordered. "Tighten the latigos on your jaws and listen to your boss and do what he tells you. Then the rest of you clear out onto the porch and stay there till we want you."

Slade's words, spoken with the authority that expects and gets obedience, stilled the clamor. Tom Mawson barked terse orders. A man darted down the steps and raced for the barn. The others tiptoed out of the room to stand in a silent cluster just outside the door. Slade walked back to the couch and gazed down at young Clate Mawson's flushed and contorted face. His own face was very grave. He bent over the wounded man, placed an ear against his chest and listened to his breathing and the jerky beating of his heart. He straightened up and faced old Tom Mawson.

"Listen, sir," he said, "your son is in mighty bad shape. The slug that went through him smashed a rib — splintered it. From what he told me and from the sound of what's going on inside him, I'm afraid the splintered end is pressing against his heart and working into the muscle as he breathes. I don't think he'll live till the doctor gets here if something isn't done."

Mawson's face went white. "Wh-what can we do?" he asked.

"Just one thing," Slade replied. "Take a gamble on killing him to give him a chance."

"What do you mean?"

"I mean," Slade answered slowly, "that he must be operated on at once. That bone splinter has to be taken out before it punctures the heart wall. If it does that there will be a massive internal hemorrhage that will almost instantly be fatal."

"But — but who's going to do it?" gasped Mawson. "Nobody here's a doctor."

"I'm not a doctor either," Slade replied, "but I've patched up quite a few folks in my time and I once saw, and helped with, just about the same kind of an operation. In that case the splintered bone was working into the lung. This is worse, but the operation should be just as easy. After all, it's a relatively simple matter; not like working on an internal organ, something only a trained surgeon could attempt. This just consists of making an incision in the chest and hauling out that splinter of bone. I haven't anything much to work with, no chloroform to put him to sleep, but I believe I can do it. I'll be honest with you, because I have no anesthetic and only a makeshift tool with which to do the cutting, the shock may kill him, but I'm positive he'll die anyhow before the doctor gets here if something isn't done. As I see it, it's the only chance he's got, but it's up to you, sir, you're his father and you have the say."

Old Tom Mawson's face was twisted in an agony of indecision. His hands balled into trembling fists, sweat glistened on his temples. He stared wildly at Slade, met his level eyes.

And something he saw in those steady eyes, now all compassion and understanding, suddenly filled the anguished father with confidence. He squared his shoulders, his hands steadied.

"Go ahead," he said in a quiet voice. "I've a notion you can do as good a chore as the doctor. Hand out the powders and we'll do whatever you say."

Slade gave the needed instructions without hesitation or indecision. "Call in some of your men," he said. "Get hot water — plenty of it — and clean clothes. Clear off a big table — the dining table will do — and lay him on it. Bring every lamp in the house and place them to throw all the light possible on the table. A man must hold each of his legs. Same goes for his arms. Mr. Mawson, you place yourself where you can grip his shoulders. He's unconscious now, but the chances are when I begin cutting, he'll snap out of it and struggle. And for God's sake don't let him get away from you or move his chest sideways while I'm using the knife. Does everybody understand what he's to do, now? Okay, get going!"

The quiet authority of his voice sent men scurrying in every direction. Soon all was in readiness. Slade drew his long bladed pocket knife and opened it.

"A devil of a tool for such a chore," he told Mawson as he thumbed the blade, "but it's got a razor edge and is first-class steel. Anyhow, it'll have to do."

He walked to the kitchen stove, in which a roaring fire was going. Removing a lid, he passed the knife blade through the flame a couple of times and waved it in the air to cool it.

"All right," he told his assistants, "you know what to do. Hang onto him no matter what happens. All set?"

He bent over the wounded man's chest and used the knife with swift, sure strokes. Clate Mawson groaned, gasped. Slade cut the flesh again. Clate screamed and struggled madly to throw himself from the table. Slade stepped back and calmly waited while the sturdy cowhands fought his desperate efforts and pinned him motionless. Clate gave a last agonized cry, went rigid and relaxed to lie without further sound or motion.

"He's gone!" panted one of the cowboys.

"No, he's just passed out again, which is the best thing that could have happened," Slade replied quietly. "We shouldn't have any more trouble with him. Steady now, I'm almost finished."

Another quick stroke of the knife and he reached deft, gentle fingers through the bloody opening. With an exclamation of satisfaction he drew forth the deadly splinter, fully a third of the rib with a needle point; he held it up for Tom Mawson to see.

"Okay," he said, "got it without doing any damage. See how his breathing has changed already. Now we'll clean the wound and pad it to check the bleeding. The rest of the rib looks all right but shaping it up is too much of a chore for me, even if I had the tools. The doctor will finish the job."

He worked on the wound for some time, surveyed the bandaging and straightened his back with a sigh of relief. He picked up the bloody section of rib and regarded it quizzically.

"Save it for him as a souvenir," he told

old Tom. "Maybe he'll want to make a knife handle of it. Isn't everybody able to claim he's carrying a hunk of himself around in his pocket!"

That broke the tension. The cowboys shook with suppressed mirth. Even old Tom indulged in a wan chuckle.

"Put a thin pillow or a folded blanket under his head," Slade directed. "Cover him well and somebody sit beside him. We won't move him till the doctor gets here. I'm ready to bet a hatful of pesos that he'll pull through."

Old Tom Mawson wiped the sweat from his face, and there was a glitter of tears in his eyes as he gripped Slade's hand.

"Feller," he said thickly, "I believe you're right. There's no use for me to try and say anything for what you did, but if you ever want a favor from me, no matter how big, I want you to ask and ask quick."

Slade smiled down at him, his even teeth flashing startlingly white in his bronzed face. "Well, sir," he said, "there's something you can do for me right now; I'd sure appreciate a bite to eat. And I'd like to put up my horse."

Mawson instantly began shouting orders to the cook. "I'll take care of your cayuse myself," he finished.

"Much obliged," Slade replied. "I'll walk out with you, though. Old Shadow is sort of shy about anybody putting a hand on him without my okay."

A moment later Mawson was exclaiming admiringly over the great black horse who accepted his ministrations with dignity after Slade formally "introduced" the ranch-owner.

With Shadow properly cared for, Slade and Mawson returned to the house. Slade examined young Clate again and was satisfied with his appearance; he seemed to have drifted into a natural sleep. Leaving him on the dining-room table with two watchful cowhands sitting beside him, Slade walked out to the kitchen with Mawson.

"And now, sir," he said as they sat down, "I'll tell you all I know of what happened up there on the rimrock trail."

As the story progressed, Mawson's lined face hardened and his frosty eyes blazed with fury. "That danged oil crowd!" he declared. "There ain't nothing they won't do when they're on the prod against you."

Slade studied him a moment. He suspected that Mawson was a leader of the cowmen of the section.

"Those fellows I saw didn't ride like oil workers," he objected.

"Oh, I don't mean the fellers who drill the wells and put up the derricks and so on," Mawson explained. "I mean the operators and their guards they hired to watch the wells — they're just paid gunmen of the worst sort — and the bunch of crippled crawlers they brought in to set up in business in that infernal town they built. It's a crowd ornery enough to eat off the same plate with a snake. And every owlhoot from the Big Bend country and Mexico and every place else makes that town his headquarters. This used to be a nice peaceable section with nice folks living in it, but now!"

"You've had trouble with the oil folks?" Slade asked.

Mawson barked at the cook to rustle his hocks and get food on the table and answered, "If ruining my grass and poisoning my stock and widelooping cows is trouble, I've had plenty of it. A whole section of my south range is spoiled. The first well a young whippersnapper named Bob Kent drilled spouted oil all over the section. And I've found plenty of my cows stretched out dead from the stinkin' stuff."

"You mean, sir, that a gas well ran wild and poisoned stock?" Slade asked.

"Ain't no gas wells so far as I've heard about," Mawson replied, "but there's oil over everything."

"Gushers, eh?" Slade commented.

"Reckon the first one Kent drilled was what they call that," Mawson said, "but it didn't last long, just a few days. Plenty of oil, but since that they have to pump it out, I understand."

Slade nodded and looked thoughtful. "A gushing well usually has one of two explanations," he remarked. "Either pressure induced by confinement in a restricted area, sometimes by a field being at the bottom of an underground slope, or the pressure exerted by a gas pocket. An extensive gas pocket may mean a gushing well for a long time, perhaps to the full extent of its producing life. The first sort experiences a swift diminishing of pressure and quickly becomes a pumper."

Mawson glanced at him curiously. "You talk like you know considerable about the oil business, son," he commented.

"Oh, I've been around a few fields in my time," Slade replied with truth. He did not explain that his experience had not been restricted to observation. Nor did he deem it necessary to explain that before joining the Rangers, he had graduated from a famous college of engineering, a profession he still intended to follow some day and the knowledge of which had more than once proved valuable in the course of his Ranger activities.

"And you're sure there are no gas wells?" he added.

Mawson shook his head.

"And still you've had cows poisoned?"

"Plenty of 'em," Mawson insisted. "The danged oil gets everywhere. The creek down there that supplies all my south pasture with water is plumb ruined. The stuff is all over the water in a thick scum and the cows won't drink it, but it seeps into the holes farther north where they do drink and it kills them."

Slade stared at the rancher, who undoubtedly believed what he said, but which to him sounded rather incredible.

"It's the ruination of this section, that infernal oil strike!"

"I'm not so sure," Slade returned quietly. "I've a notion it's liable to turn out the best thing that ever happened here."

"What's that?" Mawson demanded.

"For instance," Slade continued, "I've a notion you could use a railroad line down here."

"We could," Mawson agreed. "It would do away with a mighty bad seventy-mile drive. But we'll never get one."

"That's where you're wrong," Slade said. "I happen to know that the C. & P. has for some time been considering a line to the south and on into Mexico."

"Tarnation!" exclaimed Mawson, "it's a desert to the south of here and a mighty bad one."

"A desert provides no insurmountable obstacle to railroad building," Slade replied. "In fact, once they get over the cap rock and down to the desert floor, it makes for construction at low cost and low cost maintenance to follow. I heard the route chiefly under consideration is to the east of this valley, but with the oil field going strong and guaranteeing plenty of business for the road and a growing town right here, I predict they'll change their plans and build straight down from McCarney, coming close to the field and passing over the cap rock."

"Would make for mighty handy shipping," admitted Mawson, adding pessimistically, "but the way things are going we won't have any cows to ship by the time it gets here. In addition to the poisoning, we've had more cows widelooped in the past month than in two years before."

Slade nodded but did not comment. He was content to let the seed he had planted in Mawson's mind do a little growing.

Slade enjoyed a really excellent meal, old Tom having coffee to keep him company. He had finished eating and was rolling a cigarette when hoofs sounded outside and the white-bearded old frontier doctor from Proctor, the cattle town to the north, came hurrying in. He nodded to Mawson and the others and went to work without delay. He removed the bandages, stared at Slade's handiwork and picked up the fragment of splintered rib and turned it over in his fingers. Then he spoke to Mawson.

"Who did it?" he asked peremptorily.

"Who shot him?" Mawson replied. "I wish I knew, Doc Cooper."

"The devil with that!" snorted the doctor. "I ain't interested in who shot him. That's for you to take care of. I mean who did this chore of operating on him?"

Mawson called to Slade who still sat smoking in the kitchen. Doc Cooper started slightly as his glance took in the Hawk's towering form.

"Yes," he remarked, almost as if repeating something he had once said before, "the world lost a mighty fine surgeon when you decided to be a cowboy. Surgeon's hands, no nerves, and the guts to go through with a thing like this without hesitating." He

28

turned to Mawson.

"Tom," he said, "if you begin right now and keep on the rest of your life, you wouldn't be able to make up to this big feller what he did for you. Clate would have been dead long before I got here if it wasn't for him. As it is, I figure he'll be up and getting into more trouble by this time next month. Now clear out of here, all of you, and let me finish this chore. There isn't much but routine work to do but I don't want you in my way. You stay here, young feller," he added to Slade. "I'll need somebody to handle the chloroform and pass me things. I want to straighten out the end of the broken rib, anchor it and make sure there's proper drainage. Outside, everybody else!"

Mawson and the cowboys left the room. Doc Cooper closed both doors, turned to Slade and held out his hand.

"What in blazes are you doing over here, Walt?" he asked in low tones.

"What are you doing here, Doc?" Slade asked as they shook hands.

"Got tired of the Panhandle a couple of years back and moved down here," Cooper replied. "Figure to move to Weirton soon; most of my practice is down there of late and getting better. How's McNelty?"

"He's fine," Slade replied. "Doc, I want to ask you a few questions while I've got the chance. What's Tom Mawson's standing in this section?"

"Reckon he's just about run it for a good many years," Cooper replied as he began laying out his instruments. "He owns the best spread in the section and his neighbors look up to him. Has a hefty finger in the political pie. Honest enough, so far as I've been able to learn, and a pretty good feller, but he knows how to hate. Somebody will catch it over what was done to Clate, you can bet on that."

"Has he any bad enemies?" Slade asked.

Doc shook his head. "None that I've ever heard of, unless you want to call the oil people enemies," he replied. "He's on the prod against them for fair and it's only natural that they resent his attitude. He claims they're ruining what was a nice cow country. No doubt but the oil has played havoc with his south holding, and the same goes to an extent for another spread over to the east, the Bradded R. Grass killed, or close to it, for a couple of miles north from the creek that is their south line. And the creek surface is all covered with a thick oil scum so the cows won't touch the water."

"Mawson says cows that drank from his

waterholes farther north were poisoned," Slade remarked.

Cooper shrugged his shoulders and passed Slade the chloroform bottle. "So I've heard," he replied noncommittally.

"And what do you think of that?" Slade asked.

"About the same as you do, I reckon," Cooper answered. "Might be possible, but doesn't seem to make sense."

Slade nodded, his eyes thoughtful. "Otherwise has there been much trouble?"

"Stray shootings like the one tonight, quite a few robberies of one sort or another and plenty of cattle stolen," Cooper replied. "No doubt but the oil strike brought in a rough crowd — that town grew up almost overnight and you know what that means. Naturally all the owlhoots within travelling distance sort of congregate there. Just like it was up at Beaumont and at the Gladwell strike. The cattlemen don't like it, which isn't surprising, and blame the oil operators for everything."

"What is the operators' side?" Slade asked.

Doc shrugged again. "As I said, there have been some shootings and some payroll robberies, and a well set afire that came dang near to burning up the town. The operators got mad and hired guards to protect their

31

property, and you know the sort of hellions whose guns are for hire. The cowmen say those guards are responsible for most of the shooting and robbing and cow stealing, them or friends they brought in and tip off to what's easy pickings. No proof been advanced by either side, but that doesn't change folks' temper much."

"Plenty of trouble in the making, as I guess is to be expected," Slade agreed. "Well, we'll see."

"Oh, you'll enjoy it," Doc snorted. "You're loco as any sheepherder that ever scratched a tick, but I suppose that's why you stay on with the Rangers instead of being an engineer like your dad planned for you."

"Oh, I will be some day," Slade replied cheerfully. "You know how it was, Doc, because of the loss of our ranch due to blizzards and droughts and Dad's untimely death I was unable to take the post-graduate course I'd planned for after college. So, having worked with Captain Jim during summer vacations, I decided to sign up with the Rangers for a while. I've kept up my studies and have already gotten about as much as I'd have gotten from the post-grad. I'm about all set, but I aim to stick with Captain Jim for a while yet."

"Uh-huh, and end up like him," Doc

grunted, "a spavined old coot with the temper of a teased snake. Well, is there anything else you want to know? I've finished with this young hellion."

"One more question," Slade said. "You say Mawson's holdings run down to that creek to the south of here?"

"That's right," nodded Doc. "His and the other holding; the creek is their south line."

"And how about the land south of the creek?"

"They used that as open range," Doc answered. "It was state land, but now the oil drillers and the Weirton folks have it. Young Bob Kent, who started all this, got title to a strip first and put down the first well. He owns the land most of the town is on. I understand Mawson and the neighbors talked of getting title down there but never got around to it. Put it off till it was too late. Anything else? No? Okay, call 'em in."

THREE

After seeing to it that Clate Mawson was properly put to bed, Doc Cooper drank a cup of coffee and departed.

"No sense in me hanging around," he told old Tom. "Just keep him quiet. You can give him some broth when he wakes up. I'll drop

33

in tomorrow evening for a look at him."

Tom Mawson saw the doctor to the door and then returned to the living room. He eyed Slade a moment.

"Just passing through, son, or do you aim to stick around a while?" he asked.

"Depends," Slade returned. "I may try to tie onto a job of riding for a spell, after a while; seems to be a nice section."

"Well, if a job is what you're looking for, you can stop right now," Mawson said emphatically. "Nothing would please me better than to have you sign up with me. Not just because anything I've got you're welcome to. I really need somebody dependable to give me a hand right now. Clate getting knocked out puts me on considerable of a spot. He's just about run the spread for the past few years. Curly Nevins is my range boss, but Curly's even older than me and rather stove up. He's all right but he can't get around like he used to any more than I can and with all the trouble bustin' loose hereabouts of late it's a bit too much of a chore for a couple of old jiggers to try to handle."

"I've a notion I could do a lot worse than to sign with you and I'm likely to take you up on it," Slade replied. "First I want to ride down and look over the oil strike town and maybe just loaf around for a few days. Sort of feel the need of a rest, then we'll see."

"Okay, we'll let it go at that," Mawson agreed, "but the job is plumb wide open whenever you want it and I'd sure like to have you. So you want to look over that danged town, eh? You won't get the smell of it out of your nose for a week, and the reptiles you'll find crawling around down there smell worse than the infernal oil.

"And now I figure a mite of shut-eye is in order," he added. "I sure feel all in. You sleep here in the *casa,* son. Curly Nevins does and a couple more of the older hands. We've got lots of room and I've got no women folks here now. My wife died ten years ago and my gal is off to school. She'll be back in another week or so, incidentally. She's a fine gal, just turned twenty. Clate is a couple of years older. Okay, you take the room to the left at the head of the stairs. If you want anything just call me; I sleep at the end of the hall."

Slade got his saddle pouches and Mawson led the way up the stairs, opened the door and lighted a lamp.

"Nobody in the room next to you," he remarked. "That's the one Mary, my gal, uses when she's home. Good night, son, see you in the morning."

Slade did not go to bed at once, however. He moved an easy chair to the open window and sat down. Drawing the greasy leather cap from his saddle pouch he examined it carefully, running a finger along the ragged tear made by the bullet that knocked it off the horseman's head on the rimrock trail. There was no doubt in his mind but the torn headgear had been worn around the oil wells; it reeked of the stuff. Which, he was forced to admit, lent some credence to Tom Mawson's contention that the oil workers or their associates had had a hand in the shooting of young Clate. But the mysterious riders of the rimrock trail had been wearing rangeland garb and they rode like cowhands. Funny sort of a rainshed for a cowboy to be wearing, though. That required some explaining. Of course there was no reason why a former cowhand shouldn't be working around the wells. The pay was better than following a cow's tail and not all punchers were so wedded to range work that they wouldn't leave it even for more money. Well, maybe he would learn more tomorrow. Anyhow, it appeared things were just as lively as Captain McNelty predicted he'd find them.

Slade chuckled as he recalled the interview

that preceded his ride to Weirton Valley. Captain Jim had been in a bad temper anyhow, but when he ripped open a letter and read its contents he exploded for fair.

"A troop they want just because the danged oil strike over there is spoiling the grass!" he snorted. "And me with a section about half the size of the rest of the United States to police with not a fourth of the men needed to do the job, and trouble bustin' loose along the Border! Sheriff can't handle the trouble! Got to have Rangers to keep it down! What's Texas coming to, anyhow!"

Slade had managed to keep a grin from his lips, but he couldn't keep it out of his eyes. Captain Jim glanced up from the letter and glared at his lieutenant and aceman.

"Funny, is it?" he barked. "Well, I don't see a darn thing funny about it."

Slade tried hard to look serious and concerned, and failed. Captain Jim continued to glare and mutter. Slade decided to risk a comment. "Grass spoiled by oil the only trouble?" he asked.

"Oh, there have been a few shootings and some robberies and a lot of cows wide-looped, according to this danged thing," replied Captain Jim, slapping the letter on the table. "And it's claimed somebody set fire to a well and pretty near burned up that infernal town of Weirton — pity they didn't. The cattlemen blame the oil workers for everything that's happened and the oil workers say the cattlemen fired their well. There's a taking of sides and trouble a-poppin' generally."

"You say a well was fired?" Slade remarked, looking serious.

"That's what's claimed," said Captain Jim.

"Sort of like what happened at Batson, when a gas well ran wild and killed a lot of cattle and horses and hogs and three men. The cowmen set fire to that well, I believe."

Captain Jim nodded. "You're right, but there was no organized trouble at Batson. Captain Brooks handled that situation all right, without any help from anybody else."

"Reckon one man should be able to take care of this trouble, without any help," was Slade's laconic comment.

"Okay, you asked for it!" growled Captain Jim, "but if you come running back here with your tail on fire, don't blame me."

"I won't," Slade promised, his eyes dancing. "Well, guess I'd better get going, it's a long ride."

As Slade's tall form passed out the door, Captain McNelty had the look of a man whose burden has been considerably lightened.

"No, he won't come running back," he muttered to himself, "but before everything is finished, the seat of somebody else's pants will ring like a bell, and you can bet on that."

Still chuckling over his recollection of Captain Jim's tantrums, Slade rolled a cigarette and sat gazing at the dim glow in the sky that marked the site of the oil town ten miles to the south.

Without any preliminary warning the glow changed. An angry flare ran up the long slant of the sky. Flickering and pulsing, it blazed red against the smoke pall, paling the stars and even the silvery sheen of the moonlight. Slade leaned forward, staring at the ominous glare. His pulse quickened and his forgotten cigarette burned toward his fingers. There could be but one explanation of that leaping glow; another well was on fire.

He thought of saddling up and riding to the scene of the disturbance, but decided not to. He could hardly leave the house and get his horse out of the stable without arousing somebody and he figured the Walking M had had enough excitement for one night. He'd learn about what happened the next day.

For some time he watched the red flare throb against the sky, then he went to bed and was almost instantly asleep.

Young Clate Mawson was conscious the following morning. He was weak and in some pain but was evidently already on the mend. Slade thought it safe to question him as to how he came by his hurt.

"I hardly know what happened," he told Slade and his father. "I was coming back from Yardley on the other side of the hills after attending to that chore, Dad, when I heard a bunch riding fast behind me. As they came up I pulled aside to let them pass. Didn't think anything of it, figured it was just some of the boys from one of the spreads. When they got opposite me I whooped to them. Somebody swore, then about a dozen guns seemed to let go at once. Something that felt like a sledge hammer slammed me and I knew I was hit. I managed to get my gun out and pulled trigger once. Then I didn't know anything more till I found this feller bending over me and asking me what happened."

"You didn't get a good look at any of them?" Slade asked.

Clate shook his head. "No, I didn't have time. The feller riding in front appeared to be a big gent but I didn't notice his face. Brush on both sides of the trail there and it was rather dark. Thanks, feller, for everything; Dad told me about it."

Slade smiled and patted his hand. "Just take it easy now and you'll be okay," he said. "I'll talk to you again later."

After a late breakfast, Slade got the rig on Shadow. As he was shaking hands with Tom Mawson, a wizened old cowboy appeared mounted on a sturdy bay. It was Curly Nevins, the range boss.

"I'm heading for town, too," he told Slade. "We'll ride together. The boss wants some stuff from down there."

"They got better shops in the stinkin' hole than up at Proctor and you can get things you can't get there," old Tom explained defensively.

Slade nodded, the dancing lights of laughter in the back of his eyes, but did not otherwise comment. He and Nevins headed south on the Chihuahua.

For several miles they passed over rolling rangeland dotted with fine fat beefs. Slade commented on the excellence of the range.

"Uh-huh, it's this way clear to the hills, twenty miles to the east and forty miles to the north," Nevins replied. "After that to the north it's a regular badland. That's what

41

makes the drive to McCarney and the railroad such a tough chore."

Slade was studying the contours of the hills walling in the wide valley on the east and west. He turned in his saddle and gazed north toward the misty blue of more hills.

"This valley was once a great lake or inland sea," he remarked to his companion.

Curly Nevins shot him a quick glance. "Funny for you to say that," he commented. "That's just what young Bob Kent who drilled the first well said. He said the rimrock up there was once the shoreline and covered with all sorts of big growth, and that conditions were perfect for the makin' of oil pools."

"He was right," Slade replied.

"The way things turned out, sort of looks like he was," Nevins admitted. "Most folks and even some of his drillers, after they'd dug down better'n a thousand feet and hadn't hit anything, said he was loco, but he sure fooled 'em. I'll never forget the day that well came in and what happened afterward. I was right there when she began spoutin' and hung around the section quite a bit afterward. Was plumb interesting. Like to hear about it?"

"I would," Slade replied.

Curly Nevins was an unlettered cowhand,

but he had a gift of narration and a remark-
able memory for details. Walt Slade's quick
imagination reconstructed the story as it
fell from the old cowboy's lips until he felt
he was a spectator of the stirring events.

FOUR

"All I've got to say is that it's the locoest
deal I ever got mixed up in," declared Ayers,
the head driller. "Here we are down one
thousand, one hundred and sixty feet —
that's the last reading — and sloggin'
through a sand bank. About as much oil
under this section as you'd find in a grind-
stone. Bob Kent is plumb off his mental
reservation, if you ask me."

"His dad was one of the smartest oil men
in the business and he just about raised
young Bob in oil," objected Quales, the rigger.

"Uh-huh, and he ended up busted," replied Ayers.

"Sure, because he got into things he didn't
know anything about," said Quales. "After
all, Jasper Kent was just a driller who got
on top. He didn't have no book learnin' to
speak of. He got mixed up in business deals
and got skun, naturally. Young Bob is different. He's educated some. Don't forget, he

finished high school and had a year in college."

"That's just the trouble," Ayers declared. "Uh-huh, he goes plasterin' those hifalutin' college notions on the drilling business. Calls it scientific analysis of natural conditions, or some such durn foolishness. And what's he got to go on? Nothing but those danged hills up there he claims were the banks of a big sea once, and a salt spring he found in a cave. Nothing here to indicate an oil pool. No domes, no shale, no seepage. Scientific analysis! Blooey!"

"Suppose you'd prefer a witchin' stick," chuckled Quales.

"Don't go throwing off on witchin' sticks," Ayers returned seriously. "Remember old Rice Haggard down in the Neuces country? Haggard was ambling around with his forked stick one day, witchin' for water, and the stick dipped and dipped. Haggard said there was oil or something like it under the section. Folks laughed at him and said he was loco, but quite a few years later Haggard got Dunn of the Gladwell Company interested. They drilled right down where Haggard had done the witchin'. And what happened? One of the biggest production fields in Texas."

"Just happened," replied Quales. "And

I'm willing to bet that Dunn saw indications there before he set a bit to the soil. Nothing much Dunn don't know about the oil business. He's smart. And so is young Bob. You wait and see."

Ayers snorted and glared at the great walking beam of the rig doing its slow and ponderous dance as it drew the suspending rope back and forth across the pulley at the top of the tall derrick, churning the heavy bit into the ground far beneath the surface. From the bore came a soft and muffled sound as the drill pounded its way through the yielding sand.

"After all, Bill, it was you who was first to agree to Bob's proposition that we go into this thing on shares, receiving a percentage of any strike for our work instead of wages," Quales remarked.

Ayers grinned a trifle sheepishly. "I can't help but like the young devil," he said, almost apologetically. "And I don't forget that it was his dad who risked his life to get me out from under that walking beam when the well blew and caught fire up north of Beaumont. Jasper Kent had the burn scars he got that day on his face when he died.

"But just the same I still think Bob's plumb loco," he added.

Quales winked at Curly Nevins who

lounged comfortably in his saddle near the door of the cook shack, smoking a cigarette.

"Old Tom still on the prod?" he asked.

"Oh, he's still sort of ringey, but he's feeling better lately, seeing as you fellers 'pear to be sinking a dry hole," Nevins replied. "He figures you'll pull out soon and leave this section like it was."

"He may get a surprise," said a slender, pleasant-faced young man who stepped out of the cook shanty in time to hear Nevins' remarks. "Anyhow, there's no sense in him pawing sand like he has been just because I bought this little strip down here from the state. He doesn't need it for his cows."

"The Old Man is open range," Nevins replied. "This section down here south of the crik has always been open range and he figures it should stay that way. And anyhow, he don't want to see oil wells cluttering up the grassland. He says they mean ditches and pipe lines and bad smells and cows poisoned by gas. He figures it'll be the ruination of this section if you jiggers do happen to strike oil."

"He's all wrong," Kent said earnestly. "When we strike it'll be the best thing ever happened to the section. It'll bring folks in and money, too, plenty of it."

"That's just what the old man is scairt

46

of," Nevins explained. "He 'lows all sorts of unsavory jiggers will be troopin' in. He says Proctor up to the north of here is a nice cowtown and he don't want it spoiled."

"He needn't worry about that," Kent chuckled. "When we strike there'll be a town down here in no time."

"Uh-huh, when we strike," grunted Ayers.

Bob Kent chuckled again and did not directly answer his pessimistic driller.

"But we'll have to make good mighty soon or Mawson won't have anything to worry about," he told Nevins. "I've just about scraped the bottom of the barrel; no money to buy more casing, and the bank won't let me have any more. They say at Proctor that they've gone as far as they can with the land here for security. I've a notion if Mawson hadn't been swearing he's going to get title to the whole section as quick as he can they wouldn't have gone as far as they have."

"He's talking about it but he ain't done anything about it," observed Nevins.

"He's being foolish if he really wants the land down here," said Kent. "When we strike there'll be a quick grab for every foot between here and the desert and Mawson will find himself out of luck."

"I tried to tell him that myself, and young Clate agreed with me," admitted Nevins, "but he's bull-headed as an old shorthorn and says he'll get title to everything as soon as you fellers pull out."

Ayers suddenly cocked his head in an attitude of listening. The sound coming from the bore had changed. The silky chuffing had been replaced by a heavy thudding. The suspending rope danced and quivered.

"Rock!" grunted Ayers. "We got through that sand bank and hit rock again. Now we'll jiggle along forever and get nowhere."

Bob Kent rose from squatting on his heels. "Shut her down," he ordered. "We'll change the bit and sink new casing. Might as well eat first; chuck's about ready. Let's go wash up. Come on, Curly, and have a bite with us."

The engineer closed his throttle; the jiggling of the rope ceased, the walking beam hung motionless. The silence that followed could be felt. Curly Nevins dismounted and joined the drillers moving toward the cook shanty. They had almost reached the door when without warning there was a deafening roar.

"Look out!" yelled Kent and dived for the shelter of the shack.

The roar was followed by a terrific rattling and crashing. Tons of pipe were projected through the rig floor, up and out of the hole

48

and high into the air. The derrick went to pieces in a rain of falling iron and timbers. Then there was a black geyser that spouted two hundred feet in a wind-frayed, greasy plume. Crude oil sprayed the vicinity.

"She's in!" howled Ayers, dancing in the door of the shack. "Boys, she's in! I knew it all the time! Look at her spout! That's a gusher what is a gusher!"

The driller's excitement was contagious. The crew members howled and bellowed. Curly Nevins jerked his six-shooter and sent bullets splitting the air in every direction.

No tanks had been built for storage, Kent lacking the money for their construction, but he had shrewdly set his rig on the edge of a wide and deep hollow. Now oil was flowing a river into the depression, a natural reservoir.

While the crew cursed and toiled at the gigantic task of capping the gusher, Kent saddled his horse, which was tethered under a lean-to back to the shanty, and went racing to Proctor, the cowtown twenty miles to the north.

Two days of wild excitement followed before the gusher was brought under control by a firmly anchored valve. The great hollow was brimful of "black gold."

Meanwhile the activity around the well

was nothing to what was taking place on the flats west of the drilling. At dawn of the day following the strike a grader was cutting streets through the mesquite and greasewood. A stream of material wagons was rolling down from Proctor and from McCarney, the railroad town seventy miles to the north. The Proctor bank that had refused Kent further loans had literally handed him the key to its vault. Businessmen from Proctor and McCarney vied with one another offering Kent high rentals for plots of land on which to erect buildings. Kent rented the first lot with the stipulation that a building be started within one hour. The renter had carpenters at work within thirty minutes on a saloon!

Kent was right in his prediction relative to the land south of the creek. Before old Tom Mawson knew what was happening the whole section was grabbed off under his very nose. A forest of derricks began to rise. Kent was preparing to drill three more wells on his holdings. He was building storage tanks and pouring in material and equipment.

The saloon, as usual, was first to open for business, but other buildings were erected in mad haste. People poured in and above the trails hung an ever-present cloud of choking white dust. Huge wagons lumbered in with drilling supplies, foodstuffs, furnishings and liquid refreshment.

Came, too, the hangers-on of every new oil field to ply their questionable trades. The gamblers, the ladies of easy virtue, the dance hall characters opened up for business in tents and shacks, and did plenty.

Old Tom Mawson rode down and shook his fist under Bob Kent's unimpressed nose. "Dang you, you've ruined this country!" he roared. "I ought to shoot you! I oughta have shot you when you first showed up here! You've spoiled everything!"

"You're wrong, Mr. Mawson," Kent told him. "The time will come when you'll thank me."

Old Tom raised clenched fists and swore himself breathless. Still cursing he stormed back to his big ranchhouse to rumble and fume and glare south toward the smoke cloud that stained the clean blue of the Texas sky.

"And that's how she went," concluded Curly Nevins, twinkling his faded blue eyes at his absorbed listener.

FIVE

They had rounded a bend and before them in the distance lay the town of Weirton, a wide straggle of shacks, tents, false-fronts and somewhat more substantial buildings to the north.

One thing Slade instantly noted with interest. The land south of the flash and glitter of the wide creek running west to east boasted an elevation considerably above that of the land north of the stream. It was in the nature of a small mesa running from the creek to the desert five miles farther south. Again Slade turned in his saddle to gaze at the hills walling the valley.

"Up here must have experienced a subsidiary subsidence," he remarked to himself rather than to his companion. Nevins favored him with a blank look but Slade did not see fit to amplify the observation that was cryptic so far as old Curly was concerned.

"Hey!" he exclaimed, "look at the smoke boilin' up down there to the south! Danged if I don't believe there's another well on fire!"

"There is," Slade replied. "I was sitting in my window last night when it caught. Lit up the whole sky."

Nevins shook his head. "And they'll blame the cowmen for setting it, sure as blazes," he predicted.

"Not improbable," Slade conceded, "judging from the things I've heard."

When they first sighted the town it was about three miles distant. They spoke to their horses and the pace quickened. They had covered the better part of a mile when Nevins gestured toward the grassland flanking the trail.

"See what the old man meant when he was telling you about the grass down here?" he remarked.

Slade saw. The lush growth was changing to a crisped straggle utterly dead and drying up. Farther on the ground looked almost bare.

"This way nearly clean across our holdings which run east for better than fifteen miles," said Nevins. "More than six thousand acres of prime pasture gone to the devil. The spread to the east, the Bradded R, ain't affected much but the crik is spoiled all the way, a black scum all over it. Cows won't touch the water. And our waterholes even farther north than this are spoiled. Cows drank that water but it killed 'em. We had to fence every hole along here, which spoils more range."

Slade stared at the parched grass, a perplexed expression on his face.

"It just doesn't seem to make sense that overflow or seepage through the grass would reach this far," he protested.

"Maybe not, but there she is," Nevins returned.

"Yes," Slade agreed soberly, "there she is." For a third time he turned in his saddle to study the encroaching hills, his black brows drawing together till the concentration furrow was deep between them, a sign El Halcon was doing some hard thinking.

Passing across the arid region, they splashed through the waters of the stream, the surface of which reflected the sunlight in a rainbow bloom of color and was singularly smooth and glassy. Slade agreed that without doubt it was heavily coated with oil. After leaving the stream, the trail wound up a long and fairly steep slope to the crest of the mesa and they got a full view of the town surrounded by a forest of derricks.

"We'll drop in at the Black Gold," suggested Nevins. "That's the biggest and best rumhole in town. A purty nice feller named Wade Ballard runs it. Everybody likes Wade. Even the old man couldn't help but think purty well of him when he met him once up in Proctor. Asked him why the devil he had to set up business in such a stinkin' hole. Ballard told him he'd had saloons in various oil strike towns and always found they paid. Said all he knows is the likker business, was brought up in it by his dad. Said he worked in his dad's place in Dallas when he was only fourteen. Never got to go to school and learn anything else and that he has to set up where the money is."

"Not an illogical viewpoint," Slade admitted.

"Reckon you went to school plenty, son, judging from the way you talk," Nevins chuckled. "How the devil did you get to punchin' cows?"

"Well, reckon my case rather parallels Ballard's," Slade smiled reply. "My dad was a cowman and sort of brought me up in the business. Reckon when you've got horse hair and rope in your blood it's hard to get it out."

Nevins chuckled his understanding. A few minutes later they were threading their way along Weirton's main street which was straight and wide, differing from the usual winding continuation of a trail that formed the principal thoroughfare of the average cowtown. Slade noticed quite a few cow ponies tethered at the racks.

"Yep, the boys come here," Nevins explained. "Some friction between them and the town folks but their money is welcome and they find things livelier and more fun here than at Proctor where the old-timers run things and it's a bit on the stodgy side."

Slade nodded his understanding. Nevins pulled up in front of a rough building boasting an ornate false-front and much plate glass.

"They sure put her up in a hurry, but didn't do such a bad job of it," Nevins remarked to Slade. "Inside she's quite a joint; the mirror back of the bar came clean from Dallas."

The big room was indeed a scene of contrasts. The woodwork was raw and unpainted, the long bar of rough planks, but the back bar mirror was real French plate. The chairs and tables were new and shiny. There was a roulette wheel elaborate with carvings and decorations and the lunch counter over to one side gleamed with copper and glass.

Bottles of every shape and color pyramided the back bar. The three bartenders wore white coats and shirts and black string ties. The dealers at the card tables were garbed in somber black. A lookout on a high stool wore fancy stitched boots and had a sawed-off shotgun cradled across his knees.

Early as it was, there was a sizable crowd in the place. Most of these, Slade noted, were undoubtedly oil workers in greasy clothes and laced boots. There was a sprinkling of cowhands. Also, several gentlemen who looked like cowhands but whom, Slade quickly decided, had not for some time been on familiar terms with rope or branding iron. Soberly dressed shopkeepers and other substantial citizens completed the gathering.

Standing at the far end of the bar was a small, neatly dressed man with surprisingly broad shoulders for his height and abnormally long arms. His features were shapely and regular as is often the case in small men and his face seemed to wear a perpetual smile. His eyes were a clear blue and had a keen look about them. His hair was tawny and inclined to curl. He waved a slender hand to Nevins and nodded in a friendly fashion.

"That's Wade Ballard who owns the place, the feller I was telling you about," Nevins said to Slade, as they found places at the bar and ordered drinks.

While they were sipping their glasses, a tall, powerfully built and rather uncouth looking man with a blocky, bad-tempered face entered. He rumbled a greeting to Nevins and passed on to the far end of the bar.

"That's Blaine Richardson, a sort of salty hombre but a mighty good oil man, from what everybody says," remarked Nevins. "Guess there's nothing about the business he don't know. I understand he brought in a couple of good wells in Oklahoma and some up at Beaumont. He's brought one in here, down toward the desert. He says the natural slope of the land is toward the desert and that there should be some good drilling out there on the sands and is thinking of having a try of it. Fact is he says the real strike will be made down there where the deeper part of the pool must be."

Slade glanced quickly at his companion and then shot a glance at Richardson who, glass in hand, was talking to Wade Ballard.

"An experienced oil man you say?" he remarked. "Not just a driller?"

"Oh, I reckon he came up from a driller," Nevins replied. "Rough sort of a jigger."

Slade nodded, his eyes thoughtful.

Suddenly a heavy explosion quivered the air. The glasses jumped on the bar, the bottles rattled.

"What in blazes?" demanded Nevins.

"They're trying to blow that burning well and put out the fire," the bartender explained. "Reckon they're not having much

58

luck with it. I heard the pressure is mighty low and the fire spreads out so they can't get close enough to chuck the dynamite in the bore. All they've been doing is blow holes in the ground. Liable to have to wait till she burns down a lot. Plenty of money going up in that smoke."

"What you say we ride down and take a look at it?" Nevins suggested.

Slade offered no objection and a few minutes later found them riding across the prairie toward the great cloud of smoke that marked the burning well. More dynamite was set off before they arrived at the scene but the pall of smoke, shot through with tongues of flame, continued to foul the clear air.

They pulled up as near the well as was practical and watched with interest the activities of the workers who were engaged in an effort to extinguish the blaze.

Standing nearby was a pleasant-looking young man and an older one with grizzled hair and a worried face.

"Hi-yuh, Bob," Nevins called as the younger man glanced their way. "Come on over, I want you to meet Walt Slade, a right hombre if there ever was one. Slade, this young squirt is Bob Kent who started all this down here."

"And this is Arch Caldwell who owns that danged burning well," Kent said, nodding to his companions as they shook hands.

Slade also shook hands with the elderly Caldwell. He liked the looks of both men.

"We ain't doing any good," Caldwell replied to a question from Nevins. "Can't get close enough to place the dynamite right, and if a good wind springs up it's liable to spread to the other wells."

Slade dropped his gaze to the operator's face. "Mr. Caldwell," he said, "I've a notion I can get that fire out for you."

"What's that?" exclaimed Caldwell, staring at the ranger.

"A little trick I saw worked once," Slade elaborated, not deeming it necessary to explain that it was he who had worked the trick. "I believe I can work it here if you'll give me the chance and get together the stuff I'll need."

Caldwell hesitated, stroking his chin and still staring at Slade.

"Better let him have a try at it, Arch," urged Bob Kent. "I've a notion Slade's the sort of feller who gets things done."

"And you can say that over and double it," remarked Curly Nevins.

The stocky Caldwell shrugged his shoulders. "Okay," he consented. "You can't make things any worse, that's sure for certain. What do you want to work with?"

Slade dismounted with lithe grace, towering over the old operator. "First off," he said, "I'll need a fairly flexible steel rod about a half or three-quarters of an inch in diameter and six feet long. Then a file and a coil of fine but strong wire. The wire must be strong or something is liable to happen if it breaks at the wrong time."

"I can get all that," Caldwell said. "What else?"

Slade glanced around, nodded with satisfaction. "Kent," he said, "see that thicket over there? Looks like some young hickories are growing from a stump. There should be plenty of good straight shoots coming out of that stump. Cut me three or four and bring them here."

The young oil man hastened to obey. Caldwell had already departed in quest of the needed materials; he was back soon with all Slade had requested. A group gathered around the ranger and watched his preparations with interest.

Slade took the file and notched the steel rod at both ends. He secured the wire to one end, bent the springy rod into an arc and secured the other end of the wire. Kent meanwhile had returned with an armload of strong, straight hickory shoots. Slade cut several to four-foot lengths and carefully notched the smaller end of each.

"A bow and arrows!" chuckled Kent. "What you figure to do, feller — shoot holes in the fire?"

"Something like that," Slade replied with a smile. "Now I want dynamite, one stick at a time. I don't want a box lying around here if something should go wrong. Bring caps and fuse, too."

A workman procured one of the fat, greasy cylinders. Slade proceeded to bind it to the un-notched end of the arrow, using a length of wire to secure it firmly in place.

"Good Lord!" exploded Kent, understanding at last. "You mean to say you're going to try and shoot that thing into the well? If the wire breaks or the arrow slides sideways there won't be enough left of you to grease a gun barrel with!"

"Reckon everything will work out okay," Slade replied cheerfully as he capped the stick and secured a very short length of fuse to the cap. He drew matches from his pocket.

"Going to light the fuse?" exclaimed Kent. "Tarnation! Why not just shoot it into the fire and let the flames light the fuse? Would be a heck of a sight safer."

"Yes, but the chances are it wouldn't work," Slade replied. "There is some pressure coming out of the well and the flames are several feet above the ground. The fuse would hardly light as it whizzed through them."

"But wouldn't the jar when the dynamite landed set it off?" Kent suggested.

Again Slade shook his head. "You'll notice there's a considerable oil pool under the fire," he pointed out. "That would cushion the fall and tend to minimize the shock, unless we had the luck to drop it right in the bore, which isn't likely, and even then the rising column of oil would be very apt to toss it back before it exploded. No, the only way is to shoot it in lighted. Now all you fellows get back in the clear, just in case."

The workmen hurriedly retreated. Kent and Nevins hesitated, then also took their departure, taking the horses with them. Old Arch Caldwell stayed right where he was. Slade glanced at him questioningly.

"You think I'm going to stand back safe while another man risks his life to save my property?" the well owner growled belligerently. "I'm staying right here with you."

Slade smiled down at him approvingly and did not protest.

"Okay," he said, "you can light the fuse

after I've got the arrow on the string. That will make it easier and less chance of something going wrong."

He fitted the notched end of the arrow to the wire string as he spoke and raised the bow.

"Powder!" he said briefly.

Caldwell struck a match and applied it to the dangling end of the fuse. There was a hiss, a rain of sparks. Slade drew the death-laden arrow back its full length. Caldwell saw great muscles leap out on arm and shoulder to swell the ranger's shirt sleeve to the bursting point, for the bow was a stiff one and not easy to bend.

The bowstring twanged with a rich, deep hum. The arrow, trailing a spurtle of sparks, soared through the air and vanished in the smoke cloud over the well. Almost instantly there was a booming explosion. Smoke and flame flew in every direction, with clods of earth spurting through the fog.

"By gosh!" whooped Caldwell, "you're doing it! Look, the fire is just about half as big as it was. You've darn near got her plugged."

"Figure one more should do it," Slade replied. "Another stick of powder, somebody."

Soon he had the second charge ready. Caldwell applied the match and Slade drew back the arrow. With a click the wire slipped from the upper notch and slid down the rod. Caldwell gave a yell of consternation as the arrow twitched from Slade's fingers and the dynamite cartridge with its sputtering fuse thudded to the ground a little ways off.

Slade dived for the hissing death, seized the cartridge and hurled it toward the well with all his strength. The charge exploded in mid-air, tumbling the smoke cloud in every direction and knocking Slade and Caldwell off their feet.

"The devil with the danged thing!" gasped Caldwell as he picked himself up. "Don't take another chance, feller."

"Reckon it won't happen again," Slade replied cheerfully. "Get me another stick."

Caldwell wiped the drops from his brow with his sleeve and called for more powder. The watching group which had been augmented by new arrivals streaming out of town, stood silent and rigid as Slade prepared still another charge.

The match was applied to the fuse. Caldwell held his breath as Slade slowly and carefully drew the arrow to the head. The bow twanged, the sputtering dynamite whizzed through the air and entered the smoke cloud.

Straight and true it sped, curving downward at just the right instant.

"Got the range now," Slade observed.

The explosion followed his words. Again the smoke cloud swirled and eddied. Then it slowly drifted away, revealing a tumbled mass of earth and stone where the well mouth had been. The well was effectually capped, the fire extinguished.

A thunderous cheer arose from the watchers. Bob Kent rushed over and grabbed Slade's hand and shook it vigorously.

"Never saw anything like that before, did you, Arch?" he whooped.

"No," Arch Caldwell replied, "and I never want to see it again."

Slade passed the bow to the well owner. "Save it so you'll have it in case you need it again," he said.

"Uh-huh," Caldwell replied grimly, "but where'll I get somebody with the muscle and guts to use it?"

Others hurried forward to congratulate Slade on the success of his experiment. Among them was Wade Ballard, the owner of the Black Gold saloon.

"Where in blazes did you learn that trick, feller?" he asked wonderingly.

"Didn't learn it," Slade replied. "Just figured it out once. You know the Indians used to fire buildings with arrows in much the same way."

Ballard's keen eyes grew thoughtful. He raised a hand to smooth his tawny hair.

"I see," he said, "and the corollary is that the fire could be extinguished with an arrow."

Slade looked a little blank. "Sort of that way, if I get what you mean," he agreed.

Ballard nodded, smiled slightly and walked away. Slade heard another voice at his elbow, a growling rumbling sort of voice.

"Feller, that was smart, dang smart!" Blaine Richardson declared. "Yes, sir, a regular whizzer." He turned and shook his fist toward the north and very nearly repeated old Tom Mawson's words when he accused the oil men of shooting young Clate.

"There ain't nothin' those cattlemen won't do when they've got it in for you!"

"Do you figure the cattlemen fired the well?" Slade asked.

"Who the devil else?" growled Richardson and stalked off to join Wade Ballard. Slade followed him with a thoughtful glance.

Six

Slade and Nevins got their horses and prepared to ride back to town. Old Arch

67

Caldwell drew a bulky wallet from his pocket, met Slade's dancing eyes and thrust it back again.

"Much obliged," he said, extending his hand, "and if you should happen to be in the notion of taking a good job sort of helping me look after things around the wells, it's waiting for you."

"Thanks for the offer, sir," Slade replied. "I'll keep it in mind."

"Offer stands," Caldwell said tersely.

"That old feller is considerable of a jigger, I'd say," Curly Nevins remarked as they rode back to town.

"Yes," Slade agreed soberly. "Representative of a class that is making Texas great and will make it greater. The same breed as Tom Mawson and his kind who came into a wilderness and turned it into a garden."

Old Curly shot Slade a quizzical glance. "Got a feeling Tom Mawson wouldn't be exactly flattered if he heard you say that," he chuckled, then, his eyes suddenly thoughtful, "but again, maybe he would be."

Slade smiled and did not comment.

A moment later Bob Kent rode up behind them. "Figured to drop in at the Black Gold for a bite to eat," he remarked. "Won't you gents join me?"

"Reckon we could do worse," Slade

agreed. "Feeling sort of empty myself."

As they sat down at a table in the saloon, Slade noticed Blaine Richardson at the end of the bar talking to Wade Ballard. His bad-tempered face wore a scowl and he was gesticulating animatedly. Slade could just catch the rumble of his harsh voice.

"Reckon Blaine is sounding off about the cattlemen again," chuckled Kent. "He's sure sore at them. Fact is, I think he's always sore at everybody. He has no use for anybody's judgment but his own. When I mentioned that I rather doubted if he would strike oil out on the desert if he drilled there, he said he was drilling wells before I had any teeth and that I'd do well to keep my mouth shut and listen to people who know more about it than I do. Bill Ayers, my head driller, and Nate Persinger, Richardson's crew foreman, very nearly came to blows over it. Yes, Blaine is sure crusty. Wade Ballard sort of puts up with his yammering, but he is a free spender — stinginess isn't one of his faults — and I reckon Wade figures it's good for business to let him run on. One thing is sure for certain, nobody will ever be able to convince him the cattlemen didn't fire that well."

Slade let his gaze rest on the oil man's face. "Kent, do you think the cowmen fired it?" he asked.

Kent's face hardened a little. Before replying, he glanced at Curly Nevins, who had moved to a nearby table to speak to an acquaintance.

"Slade," he said, "I don't know what to think. Tom Mawson is sure on the prod against us. He says we ruined his grass and poisoned his cows; he's got a point there, all right; I guess we did. Fact is, I offered to pay for the cows he lost and he told me to go to the devil. As Richardson said, if the cattlemen didn't fire it, who did? But if a cowhand did the chore he knew more about the oil business than any puncher I ever heard tell of."

"You can't fire a well by setting a match to it," Slade observed inconsequentially.

"You're darn right you can't," Kent agreed. "That well was fired by some sort of a flash device triggered to go off at a certain time. Men who were working nearby said there was a sharp explosion and she cut loose with a roar. But of course, Mawson or somebody could have hired an oil worker to do the job."

Again Slade looked hard at the oil man. "Kent," he said slowly, "does it seem reasonable that a man of Mawson's standing and who is undoubtedly a shrewd article would

70

place his liberty, or even his life if somebody had been killed, at the mercy of a man he could hire to do such a chore? To say the least, he'd be putting himself in a beautiful position to be paying blackmail to somebody the rest of his life."

"It doesn't seem reasonable," Kent admitted, "but when men get really mad about something, they sometimes do foolish things."

"I agree with you there," Slade replied, "but firing the well would be nothing but a bit of petty spite work on Mawson's part. If he fired a dozen wells he still couldn't run you people out of the valley and he knows it. I talked with Mawson and he didn't impress me as the kind that would go in for petty stuff. That wouldn't be his way or I'm a lot mistaken in the man. I'll tell you something, somebody shot his son last night and came close to killing him."

"What!" exclaimed Kent. "Somebody shot young Clate?"

"That's right," Slade said, "and in my opinion if Tom Mawson felt for sure you, for instance, were responsible, his method would be to ride down here and do his best to blow you from under your hat."

"I'm inclined to agree with you there," Kent said soberly. "How did Clate come to get shot? I met him once, he's a nice young feller, more progressive than his dad. How did it happen?"

Slade related what he knew about the shooting, Kent listening with intent interest.

"And now," said Curly Nevins, who had overheard the latter part of the conversation, "and now I'll tell you why Clate doesn't happen to be all set for a burying right at this minute."

Slade had noted before that Nevins had a gift for narration; the tale lost nothing in the telling. When he had finished, Bob Kent chuckled and shook his head admiringly.

"Well," he said, "it seems you have a genius for getting in solid with everybody. First you put Tom Mawson eternally in your debt, then you go right ahead and get the oil men under obligation to you. As Arch Caldwell said, all that was needed was for the wind to freshen a bit and that whole section of the field would have very likely gone up in smoke. And you'll notice," he added significantly, "the wind is blowing pretty darn hard right now. Must be nice to have everybody thinking well of you."

"Not everybody, I'm afraid," Slade smiled. "Right now I've a notion whoever fired that well isn't feeling overly friendly toward me."

"You're right there," Kent conceded. "And it would be a good idea to keep it in mind. Whoever fired that well is a potential killer. In fact, two workers did die when the first one was fired last month."

"You may have something," Slade agreed lightly. "I'll keep it in mind."

Kent looked at him and shook his head. "I don't believe you've got a nerve in your body," he grumbled. Slade laughed and changed the subject.

"Oh, by the way," Kent exclaimed, "the excitement of the fire and everything made me forget it, but the Yardley stage over to the west of the hills was held up last night. The robbers got away with several thousand dollars. I heard Sheriff Nolan and Deputy Hawkins, who's stationed here, are over there trying to pick up the trail. I'm afraid they won't have much luck."

"Did anybody see which way the robbers went?" Slade asked.

"It happened to the west of Yardley, and the passengers said they just slid into the brush alongside the trail," Kent replied. "They said there was close to a dozen of them, all masked."

Curly Nevins glanced at Slade. "What do you want to bet that wasn't the bunch who shot Clate?" he said. "Uh-huh, I bet they

73

were headed right back here, though of course they could have kept following the rimrock and come out of the hills up around Proctor."

"You could be right about it being the same bunch," Slade conceded. "Wouldn't be surprised if you are."

It was getting along toward evening and the big saloon was filling up with a boisterous crowd. Slade noted something that gave him food for thought. The cowhands, whose number was increasing, kept strictly to themselves, and the oil workers, who were still heavily in the majority, kept away from them. The friendly merging of various groups customary to such a place was lacking; and the looks with which the two factions favored one another were anything but cordial. Slade felt that the place was very much of a powder keg with little needed to set off an explosion.

But when the row started, it was not between oilmen and cowboys but between two groups of oil workers. Slade had noticed the two groups enter the saloon, one shortly after the other, to take vacant tables that happened to be close together. The first group had waved to Bob Kent who waved back. The second passed by with a glance in his direction and a drawing together of heads. They were hardcase looking individuals dressed in working clothes, and the first group did not appear exactly tame. They interested the ranger who every now and then glanced in their directon. He noted that words were being tossed back and forth between the two tables and the voices of the speakers didn't sound exactly amicable.

Suddenly a big driller of the first group leaped to his feet with an oath. A squat, heavily built man at the other table also jumped from his chair. The two met head-on, slugging toe to toe. The heavy-set man went down with a crash, and as if his fall was a signal the other occupants of the tables were at it in a hitting, wrestling, swearing tangle.

The place was in an uproar. Men were shouting, dance-floor girls screaming, bartenders uttering soothing yells that were not heeded. The lookout was brandishing his shotgun and threatening all and sundry. Wade Ballard came boring through the mob, flinging men to right and left with surprising strength. Behind him bellowed Blaine Richardson, his face flushed a fiery red. The heavy-set man, who was wearing a gun, scrambled to his feet and charged the tall driller. And again he measured his length on the floor.

In the swift whirl of hectic action, Walt Slade's keen eyes noted what nobody else appeared aware of. The heavy-set man was riding with his opponent's awkward punches; the knockdowns were phony as a seven-dollar bill. Slade had no notion what it meant but he was instantly very much on the alert.

The heavy-set man came to his feet again, a bit more slowly, shouting curses. With a swift, smooth draw he pulled the gun at his belt and fired, seemingly point-blank at the tall driller.

Walt Slade felt the wind of the passing bullet fan his face as with a marvelous coordination of mind and muscle he went sideways from his chair. Just in time he had seen the glint of eyes in his direction, the eyes of the heavy-set man focused not on the driller but on him. And in the same flicker of perfectly timed motion, his right hand flashed down and up. The crash of a second shot caused the hanging lamps to jump. The heavy-set man howled with pain and doubled up, gripping his blood spurting hand between his knees. His gun, one butt plate knocked off, thudded to the floor a dozen feet away.

Walt Slade's voice rang through the turmoil. "Hold it!" he thundered. "Everybody where they are!" He had a gun in each hand now and the black muzzles, one wisping smoke, yawned at the battlers, who instantly stopped fighting.

Slade walked forward, his face stern, till he reached the man whose gun he had shot from his hand and who had straightened up and was cursing and wringing his dripping fingers.

"Fellow," Slade told him, "if you'd gotten away with it, that would have been very much like murder. The other man isn't armed, so far as I can see."

Before the other could reply, Wade Ballard's smooth voice echoed Slade's. "He's right, Persinger," he told the oil worker. "If it wasn't for him, right now you'd be in serious trouble. I think you'd better thank him, even if you did lose a little meat off your hand."

Persinger didn't look grateful as he glared at Slade, but apparently thought it best not to argue the point. He mumbled something unintelligible. Then Blaine Richardson's big hand fell on his shoulder.

"You're always going off half-cocked, you blasted churn-head," Richardson rumbled. "What's the matter with you fellers, anyhow?"

"And what's the matter with you, Ayers?"

Bob Kent broke in. "I'd thought you'd have better sense."

Ayers scowled at his erstwhile opponent. "That danged grease monkey was talking out of turn, that's all," he growled.

"About what?" demanded Kent.

"About you eating with a couple of cowmen," Ayers replied. "I figured it wasn't any of his business and told him so. He called me a name I don't take from nobody."

Kent turned to Slade who had holstered his guns. The Hawk's eyes were dancing with laughter. Despite the grim role he himself had very nearly played, he saw a humorous angle in the final outcome of the devilish scheme. He pictured the utter bewilderment enveloping Nate Persinger's mind as he tried to figure out how the carefully planned attempt had missed fire. It was good as a play!

"Everybody's loco," Bob Kent disgustedly declared.

Wade Ballard took charge of the situation. "All right, you fellers, straighten up the tables and chairs and try and behave yourselves for a change," he told the battered warriors. "Come on to the back room, Persinger, and I'll bandage your hand."

The fighters, looking a bit sheepish, cleaned up the mess they'd made and sat down. Persinger, with a scowl at Slade, picked up his smashed gun, jammed it savagely in its holster and followed Ballard. Slade and Kent went back to their interrupted meal. Curly Nevins stared at Slade and shook his head.

"That was shooting!" he remarked. "I never saw you pull that iron. One second it was leathered and the next it wasn't, and you pilled trigger right as it cleared. Slade, is there anything you ain't tops at?"

Slade chuckled and ordered more coffee.

Bill Ayers, the driller, came over to the table. "Much obliged, feller," he said to Slade. "I reckon you saved me from getting an airhole in my hide."

"You're darn right he did," said Kent. "There's room at the next table now. Suppose you boys come over here for the rest of the evening; I don't want any more trouble."

Ayers agreed and he and his companions occupied a table some distance from the Richardson group. Nate Persinger reappeared, his hand bandaged, Blaine Richardson accompanying him. Richardson sat down with his men, apparently to keep an eye on them. The Black Gold, which had been rather subdued for a few minutes, quickly regained its former fair imitation of

79

bedlam.

Kent and Nevins animatedly discussed the recent events, but Slade sat silent, occupied with his own thoughts. What was back of it all, he wondered. There was not the slightest doubt in his mind but that the slug had been intended for him. The whole thing had been elaborately planned with attention to the smallest details. Start a row with Kent's drillers — it was common knowledge that there was bad blood between the two outfits — and under cover of the rukus pull off a nice cold-blooded murder which on the surface would have every appearance of being a deplorable accident. The affair had been handled neatly, and to all appearances nobody but himself and the instigators of the attempt had the slightest notion of what had been intended. Persinger had played his part adeptly. Bill Ayers, Kent's head driller, possessed the usual fighting skill, or lack of it, of his class. Roundhouse punches thrown at random, easy for a man with even a smattering of the art of self-defense at his command to avoid. Persinger on the other hand undoubtedly knew how to use his fists and how to exploit the other man's lack of knowledge to the best advantage. He had faked the knockdowns in a very convincing manner. Apparently getting the worst of the fight it was not unnatural that he would lose his head and go for his gun; such things often happen and in such a community an accident, while regrettable, would be regarded lightly. Yes, the whole affair had been carefully thought out and expertly staged.

The question that puzzled the ranger was what was back of it? Bob Kent had intimated that Blaine Richardson nursed an almost insane hatred against cattlemen, but Slade felt it was ridiculous to think that Richardson would go in for such an elaborately planned killing just to glut his hate. It just didn't seem to make sense. Revenge for the role he played in extinguishing the burning well? If that was the motive, it would seem to let Richardson out. An oil-man himself, Richardson would hardly go around setting fire to wells unless he was a pyromaniac, which Slade doubted. Hatred or revenge seemed hardly the answer.

The logical assumption, Slade concluded, was that somebody for reasons unknown had decided that his elimination was necessary. Which predicated something going on that must be concealed at all hazards. Had he been recognized as a ranger? Not impossible. Or as El Halcon, an outlaw all set to horn in on somebody's good thing? That also was possible. But what was it his presence in the section jeopardized? He'd just have to wait and follow the course of events. What he hoped more than anything else was that he had been able to put over his own act to an extent that neither Persinger nor whoever else was in on the plot realized that he had caught on to the fact that he was the intended victim. Slade believed he had put it over.

SEVEN

It was late when old Curly Nevins finally decided to call it a day. "Coming back to the spread with me?" he asked Slade.

"Guess I might as well," the ranger replied. "I want to see how Clate is making out."

A few miles north of the creek, Nevins turned into a narrow track that joined the Chihuahua. "This is a short cut which will miss that big bend and knock off quite a few miles," he explained. "It isn't bad going and the moon will be up in a little bit."

They had covered a couple more miles when Nevins uttered an exclamation. "Don't I hear horses coming this way?" he asked.

Slade listened intently. "You hear more than horses," he said. "You hear cows, a lot

82

of them, and horses with them, coming fast."

"What in blazes!" sputtered Nevins. "Nobody's got any business running cows down here at this time of night."

Slade glanced around. Not far to the left of the trail was a belt of thicket. To the east was open prairie. "Into that brush over there till we see what's going on," he told his companion.

"You think . . ." Nevins began as they turned from the trail.

"Don't take time to think now," Slade broke in. "Come along!"

Muttering under his breath Nevins followed the ranger into the growth. They halted where they could look across the trail but not be seen from it.

"Be ready to grab your horse's nose if he should take a notion to neigh," Slade warned.

The drumming of many hoofs grew louder and louder. Suddenly a little distance out on the prairie a dark mass came into view, veering south by east. It quickly resolved into a large herd of cattle travelling at top speed. Short, querulous bleats burst from the laboring throats of the sweating cows. Their breath whistled through their flaring nostrils.

Slade's face set in grim lines. No legitimate riders would be running the fat off stock like that.

On came the herd. Now the attendant horsemen were clearly visible. Slade counted nine altogether. The cows were being shoved, close-bunched, across the prairie, held in line by expert point, swing and flank riders.

Slade sensed rather than saw Nevins reach for his gun. Instantly his fingers clamped the other's wrist and held it powerless.

"Lemme go!" demanded the range boss in a fierce whisper. "Those are the old man's cows."

"Hold it!" Slade whispered back. "There are nine of the hellions and they're scattered. We wouldn't have a chance. Hold it, I tell you, this will take some thinking out. Let them get past and then we'll figure something."

Nevins swore under his breath but his tense muscles relaxed. Slade let go his wrist and together they watched the herd thunder past under a film of dust that glinted silver in the pale moonlight.

"It's the beef herd from the middle pasture," Nevins breathed. "All ready for the trail the first of the week. The old man can't afford to lose those cows. Blazes! There were two night hawks riding herd on 'em. I wonder what happened to those boys."

Slade did not answer, but he had an unpleasant premonition that the Walking M was short a couple of hands. His eyes were cold in the moonlight, his face bleak as the granite of the rimrock trail.

The drumming of hoofs was dimming, the herd growing shadowy in the distance. "Listen," Slade told his companion, "they're heading for the hills over to the east, don't you figure?"

"That's right," answered Nevins. "Those hills are all cut with canyons and draws where the ground's all rocks. They could slide into any one of them and there's no trailing them once they get there."

"So I figured," Slade said. "Now here's what we'll do. You ride to the ranchhouse fast as you can and rouse up the hands. I'm going to try and keep those cows in sight. They'll never attempt to run them across the desert to the Rio Grande in the daytime, that's sure for certain. They'll hole up somewhere in the hills a bit south of here. If I can find where they're holding the cows we should be able to hit them where it hurts. That's the only chance I can see."

"Yes, but you'll be taking one heck of a risk, trailing those sidewinders," Nevins protested. "They'll be almost sure to spot you and if they do it will be curtains for you."

"I'll risk it," Slade replied. "Get going. They won't see or hear you now, and I've got to drift after them or they're liable to give me the slip."

Sputtering profanity, Nevins sent his horse northward at a gallop. Slade spoke to Shadow and the great black moved out onto the prairie at a smooth running walk.

Slade felt that at a distance, from which the dark mass of the herd could still be seen as a moving shadow in the dim light, a single horseman very likely would not be noted, even if the rustlers were keeping a watch behind them, which he thought improbable under the circumstances. At any rate he determined to take the chance of operating on that premise.

Mile after mile Slade trailed the fleeing herd across the rangeland, with the rugged battlements of the eastern hills drawing nearer and nearer, and nothing untoward happened. But now a fresh problem presented itself; the east was graying and soon the wan glow cast by the overcast moon would be replaced by the light of day, in which it would be impossible for him to avoid detection by the rustlers. Anxiously he watched the pale gray brighten. It was going to be a race between the strengthening light and the arrival of the herd at the hills.

Slade could now see that Curly Nevins hadn't exaggerated in describing the inhospitable terrain. Unlike the massive range to the west, the eastern uprisings were honeycombed with canyons and draws and gorges yawning like the black mouths of caves. A perfect hole-in-the-wall country. He scanned the terrain ahead for some grove or thicket behind which he might find temporary concealment; but the grassland rolled smoothly to the edge of the broken ground. And the sky was steadily brightening.

But now the herd was close to the hills, the wideloopers pushing it hard, their attention concentrated on the business of reaching shelter before daylight. With a sigh of relief, Slade saw the cows streaming into the dark mouth of a canyon. Soon the last laboring back had vanished in the gloom. He slowed Shadow to a walk. It was imperative that his quarry should get some distance up the canyon before he entered it.

It was uneasy riding across the open ground in the strengthening light of dawn. At any moment the black gorge mouth might belch rifle fire he would see but very likely would not hear, a slug travelling somewhat faster than sound. He heaved a deep sigh of relief when he reached the canyon without incident. It was brush grown with a fairly open space along the south wall; the floor was hard packed and stony. A posse riding in pursuit of the wide-loopers would hit the right trail only by sheer luck.

If the herd had continued into the canyon it must now be some distance ahead of him; but had it continued? It was with considerable qualms that he sent Shadow into the still gloomy opening.

Slade rode at a slow walk, listening and peering. Before him the path stretched silent and deserted in the growing light. No imprint of a passing hoof was left on the stony soil, but an occasional broken twig or a branch stripped of a few leaves told him he was on the right track.

Again he rode for miles, the gorge boring through the hills in a southeasterly direction, doubtless to open onto the arid lands to the south. Nothing broke the silence, nowhere was there a hint of sound or movement, but Slade knew he was on the tail of the herd. The canyon walls were sheer, to the right an unbroken line of beetling cliffs, on the left a stand of heavy growth.

The sun was well above the horizon when he reached a spot where the side wall was slashed by a much narrower gorge or crevice also heavily brush grown. Through the stands of growth ran a ridge of stony ground some twenty feet in width where only a straggle of bushes found rootage. Slade pulled to a halt. On ahead there were still signs of the recent passage of horses or cattle, but he knew he could not be any great distance from the south end of the gorge. He was convinced that the rustlers would never attempt to run the cattle, which now must be on the verge of exhaustion, across the desert during the blazing daylight hours. They'd never make it to the Rio Grande, nearly twenty miles away. They must hole up somewhere till nightfall and this break in the canyon wall was the first indication of what would provide a hide-out. He studied the growth ahead and tried to put himself in the place of the wideloopers. Guarding against the chance of a pursuit hitting on the particular canyon they entered, would it not be logical that they would make a false trail to lead the pursuers astray? With signs of recent passage still before them, a hurried posse might well ride on to the mouth of the canyon and then hopelessly lose the trail on the sands.

Anyhow, Slade had a decided hunch that the herd had turned off into the side gorge. Putting the theory to a test he veered Shadow into the opening and rode slowly, scanning the ground and the brush on either side. He uttered an exultant exclamation. Cattle had passed this way, and recently.

Now what should he do? Ride back to the canyon mouth and await the arrival of the Walking M bunch? Seemed the sensible thing to do. But if he was making a mistake and the cows were not holed up in this infernal crack, the wideloopers would very likely get in the clear. And if he continued through the crevice he would quite probably run into the whole gang. Also, they might very well hear him coming. No matter what he did, he risked being impaled on one or the other of the horns of the dilemma.

As he hesitated, appraising the situation with a concentration that amounted almost to mental agony, he heard a sound ahead, a faint clicking sound. Again it came, louder, undoubtedly a horse's iron striking against a stone. Slade jerked Shadow sideways and sent him into the growth that flanked the stony ridge, regardless of thorns and raking branches. Not until he was sure he could not be seen from the open ground did he pull the big horse to a halt.

"Don't go singing any songs!" he whispered as he dismounted. Careful to make no sound he stole back on foot till he could see through a final fringe of branches. The steady clicking grew louder. Another moment and seven men rode down the gorge toward the main canyon. It was shadowy in the crevice and Slade could catch only an indistinct view of their features. He watched them dwindle away until the growth hid them. Then he proceeded to take stock of the situation.

He had counted nine men pushing the herd across the prairie. So unless there had been more of the gang waiting in the hole-up, which he doubted, only two had been left to ride herd on the stolen cattle. The odds weren't so bad. Doubtless the others would not return until nightfall; but then again they might be gone only a short time. Slade resolved to take a chance on recovering the herd. He debated whether to ride farther and decided not to. It was likely the cleft was of no great depth and sounds would carry a long way between the echoing walls. Leaving Shadow where he was, he stole forward on foot, pausing often to peer and listen. He had covered less than a fifth of a mile when he heard, only a short distance ahead, the bleat of a steer. Redoubling his caution he crept on. Abruptly the gorge widened. Shafts of sunlight poured into its depths. Slade left the open space and wormed his way through the growth. Before a last straggle he paused, parted the branches carefully and peered out.

Directly ahead was an almost circular bowl walled on three sides by cliffs. There was very little brush and the ground was carpeted with grass. Near a trickle of water the weary cows were grazing. And a little to one side, two men moved about a small fire of dry wood. One was short and solid-looking, the other lean and scrawny. They were within easy shooting distance from where Slade crouched in the brush.

Slade pondered what his next move should be. The two men were proven thieves, quite likely murderers as well. They certainly deserved no quarter; he would be justified in blasting them from cover. But he was a peace officer and the stern code of the peace officer forbade such action; he would have to take his chance in the accepted fashion. Loosening his guns in their sheaths he stepped from the brush. His voice rang out, "In the name of the state of Texas! You are under arrest!"

The two outlaws whirled at the sound. For an instant they stood rigid, then they leaped apart and went for their guns.

Back and forth across the clearing spurted the wisps of blue smoke. The canyon walls rocked to the crash of the reports.

EIGHT

One sleeve hanging in ribbons, bullet holes through the crown of his hat, a red trickle running from his left hand, Walt Slade lowered his guns and peered through the drifting fog at the two bodies sprawled beside the fire. He walked forward, gun ready, but the outlaws were dead.

Sure that there was nothing more to fear from them, he gave the bodies a swift but thorough once-over. They were hard-case individuals, typical of the Border outlaw clan, their faces blotched by heavy drinking, their features coarse and scarred. Salty and brainless was his verdict. Filled with reckless courage and unhampered by morals of any sort, but capable only of carrying out orders and leaving somebody else to do the thinking for them.

Their pockets divulged nothing of significance save a rather large sum of money, but the pockets themselves of the scrawny man interested Slade. The seams were packed with a greasy grit. Undoubtedly the man bad spent considerable time around the oil wells. Which was interesting. So much so that he ripped one of the pocket linings out and stowed it away.

Slade wasted no time retrieving Shadow. Then he rounded up the cattle and headed them back down the gorge. Managing five hundred head, more or less, of stock was a hefty chore for one man, and had not the cows been too worn out to offer more than token objections, even El Halcon could not have done it. As it was, he finally got them to the main canyon and plodding in weary disgust for its mouth. Once out on the prairie the going was easier for the cattle slogged on toward their accustomed feeding grounds.

He had the herd less than two miles outside the canyon when he perceived a body of horsemen riding swiftly from the northwest.

"Now if they're just the Walking M bunch headed this way, everything is fine and dandy," he told Shadow. "But if they happen to be those widelooping gents coming back for something they forgot the only thing we can do is leave the cows and run for it."

Very quickly, however, he recognized the blocky form of old Tom Mawson riding at the head of his men. Ten minutes more and the group circled the herd and pulled up alongside the ranger, swearing in amazement and volleying questions.

"Slade," demanded Curly Nevins, when the babble had somewhat abated, "how the devil did you do it?"

"Oh, I just pointed out to those jiggers that it was wrong to steal and the only thing for them to do to make things right was send the cows back to their rightful owner," Slade replied without the trace of a smile, and added grimly, "I understand there's a deputy sheriff stationed at Weirton? Well, I'll give him the lowdown how to get to a crack back in that canyon straight ahead to the east. He'll find a couple of bodies he may want to look over."

His hearers stared at him in silence, then old Tom Mawson said heavily, "Son, it seems I keep getting deeper in your debt all the time."

"How about those two night hawks Curly mentioned?" Slade asked.

Mawson's face hardened and his tired old eyes were filled with pain. "I dunno, but I'm scairt they're both done in," he replied. "They hadn't showed up when we left. I

95

sent a couple of boys galloping over to the pasture to find out. Curly figured the rest of us had better hightail straight down here to lend you a hand. Guess it wasn't necessary."

The cowboys took over the chore of shoving the herd along, with old Tom supervising. Curly Nevins dropped back alongside Slade.

"You did the old man another hefty favor today," he remarked. "He couldn't afford to lose those cows right now. It would have hit him hard."

"Had a notion he was pretty well fixed — he owns a mighty nice piece of property," Slade replied.

"That's right," admitted Nevins, "but you'll understand what I mean when I say he's land and cattle poor right at this time. You know the longhorn market has been falling off bad during recent years. There just isn't any demand for the kind of meat they provide. So a couple of years back the old man decided to bring in blooded stuff and improve his stock, which was a good notion all right. He bought a big herd of Herefords and Anguses to breed with his longhorns. It'll pay off, but it cost plenty. He borrowed money from the Proctor bank, with the spread as security to do it. This herd was ready to run to the railroad next week, to bring in the money to pay off a note that falls due the first of the month."

"Afraid he'll have to wait a week till they get back the fat those hellions run off them," Slade interpolated.

"You're right about that," agreed Nevins, "but thanks to you he's got 'em to ship. He'd had to do some tall scratching if he'd lost 'em. They're the very best beefs we could comb out. We've lost plenty of stuff during the past few months, a little bunch here, a little bunch there, but they mount up dang fast. Reckon we sort of got caught with our guard down because the hellions had always operated that way or we'd have kept a better watch on the herd. This is the first time they really went for something big. You sure handled it smart, feller, but it's a pity we didn't get there in time to wipe out the whole nest of snakes. Maybe it's better the way it worked out, though; if we'd met 'em head on we'd been liable to lose some men, which is worse than losing cows. I'm scairt we're short a couple as it is."

However when they reached the ranch-house they learned it wasn't quite that bad, though bad enough. One of the men sent to see about the night hawks rode out to meet them.

"Jess Rader was killed," he said, "but Sam

Price was just shot through the shoulder and creased purty bad. We've got him in the *casa* and Doc Cooper is working on him. Sam said they never had a chance. The devils cut loose on them from a thicket close to the pasture and mowed 'em down. Snake-blooded hellions! And you did for two of them, feller? That's fine. Hope you get a chance at the rest, and I hope I'm along to see it."

Doc Cooper reported that the wounded cowboy should pull through all right, barring complications. "I put him in the room with Clate so they can keep each other company," he announced. "Go in and tell him you sort of evened up the score, Slade. It will make him feel better."

Price did feel better when he heard the news. His wound was painful and he had lost considerable blood but he looked tough as rawhide and Slade felt he'd recover without any trouble.

"We're getting a pretty good sizing up as a hospital here," young Clate Mawson chuckled weakly. "Space for about one more bunk. Anybody want to make reservations?"

"Hope we managed to keep it empty," Slade replied with a smile.

"Uh-huh," young Mawson agreed soberly. "There's room for another 'bed' alongside the one poor Jess Rader will sleep in up on the hill. Hope we can keep that empty, too.

"Glad Mary will be home before long," he added in more cheerful tones. "Mary's my sister, you know, and a plumb fine gal. She'll look after Sam and me all right. Takes a woman to make a man feel comfortable and satisfied when he's hogtied in bed like we are."

Old Tom stuck his head in the door. "Chuck's on the table," he announced.

As soon as he had finished eating, Slade rose to his feet. "I'm riding to town to see the deputy."

"No need to," Mawson said. "Soon as we got here I sent one of the boys to tell him. He should be there about now, been gone an hour and a half."

Slade stared at him. The rancher's well-intentioned blunder had nicely scrambled all his carefully thought out plans.

"What's the matter, son?" Mawson asked. "Did I do something wrong?"

"Don't you see it, sir?" Slade patiently explained. "The rest of those hellions will be coming back to the canyon tonight to run the cows across the desert to Mexico. I had planned on having the deputy get a posse together and ride there in the hope of dropping a loop on the lot of them. Now

I've got to hightail back to that canyon to intercept the deputy and your hand before they find themselves in a hornet's nest. They may have started out at once and it's a lot shorter ride from Weirton to that canyon than it is from up here. If they barge into that bunch unexpectedly we'll be short a couple more."

"By gosh! I never thought of that," exclaimed Mawson. "But I got a better idea; we'll all ride down there. I'm itching for a crack at those devils."

"Guess that will be best," Slade agreed. "Let's go!"

Ten minutes later the posse, more than a dozen strong, thundered off across the prairie.

It wanted two hours of sundown when they reached the canyon mouth, but Slade advised caution. "I don't think they'll get here this early, but we can't afford to take chances," he said. "Everybody keep their eyes skinned and their ears open."

However, they met nobody in the canyon. They rode up the cleft a ways and left the horses in a thicket with a man to guard them. Careful to make no sound, they covered the rest of the distance on foot, hearing nothing and seeing nothing Pushing through the last belt of growth they peered into the clearing. It lay silent and deserted. The two bodies were nowhere in sight.

With a muttered oath, Slade strode from concealment and to the spot where he left the dead men. Only a few blood stains on the grass showed where they had lain.

"Maybe Pete and Deputy Hawkins got here first and packed 'em off," old Tom hazarded.

"Impossible," Slade replied. "We would have met them on the way out."

"Then what the devil does it mean?" sputtered Mawson.

"It means," Slade said grimly, "that either Pete or the deputy talked where the wrong pair of ears was listening. Somebody hightailed out of town ahead of them and packed the bodies away. Would appear somebody in Weirton was mighty anxious to make sure they wouldn't be taken to town where they might be recognized."

"I always said all the thieves in this end of Texas congregated in that town!" fumed Mawson.

"It's beginning to look like they work out of there, all right," Slade conceded. "Well, there's nothing we can do here; we might as well head for home."

They had covered something less than a

mile down the main canyon and were nearing a bend in the brush-flanked trail when Slade abruptly held up his hand.

"Hold it!" he said. "Horses coming. Get set, we're taking no chances."

The posse jostled to a halt and sat with guns ready for instant action. The beat of hoofs loudened, approaching at a steady, purposeful pace. Another moment and two horsemen bulged around the bend, each leading a mule. They pulled up looking considerably startled at the array of hardware facing them.

"Oh, tarnation!" snorted Mawson. "It's just Sid Hawkins and Pete. Turn around and go back where you come from, you terrapins, you're too slow to catch cold!"

Questions and explanations followed. The deputy swore in weary disgust. "Those danged sidewinders always outsmart everybody," he declared. "I don't know what this section's coming to!"

"Anyhow you can both thank whatever looks after you that there's somebody in the section with brains," Mawson told them. "If it wasn't for Slade you'd be using those mules to pack your own carcasses back to town."

Pete and the deputy were thankful and said so. Slade queried the cowhand.

"Where were you when you relayed the information to Hawkins?" he asked.

"In the Black Gold — that's where I found him," Pete replied. "Nobody told me to keep it quiet and I reckon everybody around heard what I said."

"And what did you do after you spoke to Hawkins?"

"We had a couple of drinks and Sid had something to eat," Pete replied. "Then we rustled up the mules and started out. Figured we could make it before dark. I'm sorry, feller, but I didn't know you wanted it kept quiet."

"Just one of those things," Slade told him. "And the way it worked out nothing bad happened, which was more than I'd expected for a while. Lucky you decided to eat first and take your time, otherwise things might have turned out differently."

"You're dang right," growled Tom Mawson. "Now everybody might as well go home."

It was late when they finally got back to the ranchhouse and Slade went to bed without delay, too tired to even think.

He did plenty of thinking the following morning, however, as he placed the greasy cap and the ripped-out pocket side by side and gazed at them through the haze of his cigarette smoke. Undoubtedly the wearer of the cap and the dead owner of the pocket had spent considerable time around the oil wells. And the spiriting away of the two bodies was plenty significant. Somebody was extremely anxious that they should not be put on exhibition in Weirton and that their association with somebody would not come to light. Did it tie up with the attempt on his life in the Black Gold? Slade felt that indirectly it did.

But there was a perplexing loose thread banging about that refused to take its proper place in the pattern. Look for the motive, say the rangers. Men seldom do anything without a motive. Learn the motive and the trail to the quarry is wide open. Slade could not conceive of what the motive back of the attempt was.

Assuming for the sake of the argument that somebody had recognized him as a ranger, was it logical to believe that an outlaw band would seek to kill him just because he might be a potential threat to their rustling activities? Slade did not think so. Killing a ranger was a serious matter and usually fraught with dire consequences. The hunt for the killers would go on relentlessly and never cease until they were brought to justice. Would the proceeds from the theft of a few cattle, or even a great many cattle, warrant such a risk? Definitely not. No! Somebody with brains, cold courage and a callous disregard for human life was playing for high stakes.

The stakes? Walt Slade had not the slightest notion what they could be. But he did have a hunch that in some way they were connected with the Walking M spread.

NINE

After they finished eating, Slade and old Tom sat on the veranda and smoked. Finally Mawson asked a question, "Well, son, are you going to stay on for a while and help me run the dang place?"

"Yes, on a condition," Slade replied.

"What's the condition?" Mawson asked curiously.

"That I be allowed to handle things as I see fit with no interference from anybody," Slade explained.

"Done!" old Tom said. "That's the kind of talk I like to hear. You're in charge from now on."

"Okay," Slade smiled, rising to his feet, "and now I'm going to take a little ride and look things over."

Getting the rig on Shadow he rode south

by a little east. He quickly decided the spread was a comparatively easy one to work. It was roughly a twenty by fifteen mile rectangle. Chaparral growth was sparse and the only real combing necessary would be in the canyons and gorges slashing the eastern hills that walled the Bradded R, the other holding that ran down to the creek. Being open range, the stock of the outfits would mingle. He observed several small streams that flowed south to join the creek that Curly Nevins said flowed from under a cliff of the western range to cross the valley and enter one of the canyons cutting through the hills to the east. Riding steadily, he finally reached the first of the fenced waterholes. He pulled up and studied the water. It was crystal clear with no scum on the surface. Evidently the hole was fed by a spring.

Slade dismounted and climbed the barbed wire fence. With the greatest care he examined the stones at the water's edge. Finding nothing of an ominous nature, he dipped a handful of the water and tasted it; it was pure and sweet, no taint, no acidity, and no bitterness. Dipping another handful he drank a little, not much, and climbed out of the enclosure.

"No, you don't get any," he told Shadow.

"You'd be sure to drink too darn much. If I happen to be wrong, and I don't think I am, what I swallowed won't give me any worse than a few belly cramps but I'll bet you my hat against your next nosebag that I won't feel a single pain."

Shadow snorted and refused to take the bet. With a chuckle, Slade forked him and rode south. When he reached the oil scummed creek he again dismounted. The creek at this point flowed in a shallow gorge, down the slightly sloping wall of which it was possible to climb. Slade scrambled down and squatted at the water's edge. The reek arising from the stream was very strong; no wonder cows refused to drink it. He turned his attention to the jagged stone that formed the bank. It was cracked and seamed and fissured. Slade instantly recognized it as shale and typical of an oil producing region. For some time, he examined the stone, his black brows drawing together. Finally he climbed back to the prairie and stood gazing north. The valley undoubtedly sloped from north to south, which lent credence to Bob Kent's theory that the oil pool would be found underlying the mesa. Well, in Kent's case, practice had overshadowed precept: Kent did strike oil. Slade's eyes followed the contours of the hills from north to south and he shook his head in a puzzled fashion. Next he studied the almost barren wide band of rangeland extending north from the creek, and again he shook his head. To all appearances, oil seepage was killing the grass roots, but he still couldn't understand how the seepage continued for such a distance. Mounting Shadow he rode west till he reached the Chihuahua Trail. Fording the stream he headed for Weirton.

It was pretty well on in the afternoon and he decided a bite to eat wouldn't go bad. He entered the Black Gold and saw Bob Kent eating a meal at a table. The oilman waved a greeting.

"Come on and partake of a surrounding," he invited.

Slade accepted and sat down on the opposite side of the table. Kent beckoned a waiter and Slade gave his order.

"Blaine Richardson has started drilling a well out on the desert," Kent announced. "He says he's going to bring in a gusher that will make things up here look picayune. Darn it, maybe he will!"

"How about the well he drilled down on the south end of the mesa, was that a gusher?" Slade asked.

Kent shook his head. "Nope, it's a pumper like the rest of them," he replied. "The only gusher brought in here was my first strike, but the pressure eased off fast. One of the funniest manifestations I ever ran up against. Almost overnight the pressure decreased to only a slight flow and we had to start pumping. Most unusual, so far as my experience goes. The same holds good for every other well, practically no pressure at all."

Slade nodded, his eyes thoughtful.

"Richardson says," Kent continued, "that the reason is that the real oil pool is somewhere down to the south of here and that what we're getting is just the back-flow under pressure from the big reservoir beneath the desert. He says I'm wrong about this section and that the only part ever under water was the desert."

Walt Slade gazed curiously at the oilman, apparently started to speak and then changed his mind and commented only with a nod. A moment later he asked a question. "Kent," he said, "I understand you had a year in college, is that right?"

"Yes, that's right," Kent replied.

"And didn't you get any geology and petrology, the science of rocks?"

"I got some geology, but not much," Kent admitted. "Enough to give me my notion about this valley, but that's about all."

Again Slade's only comment was a nod.

"Everybody's talking about how you downed those two cow thieves and saved Tom Mawson's herd," Kent commented. "Arch Caldwell says if there were more cattlemen like you in the section there wouldn't be any trouble."

"Perhaps," Slade smiled, "but right now I wouldn't want to bet on it."

Kent glanced at him questioningly, but the ranger did not see fit to amplify his remark.

With a sigh of contentment, Kent pushed back his empty plate. "Well, got to be getting back on the job," he observed. "They're putting the finishing touches on a new storage tank over by my Number Three well."

Wade Ballard, the owner, smiling pleasantly, came over bringing drinks on the house. "You did a fine chore the other night, Mr. Slade," he congratulated the ranger. "I've a notion the loss of that herd would have hit Tom Mawson pretty hard right now."

"I suppose the loss of five hundred head of prime stock would hit any cattleman pretty hard," Slade replied. "At the current prices it would amount to around ten thousand dollars."

"And that's a lot of pesos," Ballard said

and went back to the bar.

"Wade's inclined to think Richardson may have the right idea about drilling down on the desert," Kent observed. "He told me an experienced oilman, an engineer, who came down from the Spindletop field last month to look things over agreed that Richardson was correct when he said the desert was the only part of this section ever under water, that down there was the inland sea and not up here, as I figured."

Slade glanced up quickly. "Did you talk with that engineer?"

"Nope, I was up at Proctor that day and didn't meet him," Kent answered. "Well, I'll have to be going; see you soon."

For some time after the oilman departed, Walt Slade sat smoking. Now and then he glanced toward where Wade Ballard stood at the end of the bar, and his eyes were thoughtful. Finally he pinched out his cigarette, nodded good-bye to Ballard and headed back for the Walking M.

It was late when Slade reached the ranchhouse, the front of which was dark save for a single lamp turned low in the living room, doubtless left for his convenience. After stabling Shadow he sat in the living room for some time, smoking and thinking. After a while he blew out the lamp and groped

111

his way up the dark stairway. Reaching the upper hall he located the doorknob, turned it and stepped into the room, and halted, staring.

The room, with the window shades drawn, was brightly lighted. On the bed sat a girl clad in a revealing silk nightgown. She was a rather small girl with big blue eyes and curly brown hair through which she was, at the moment, running a comb. The comb stopped moving and she stared, looking quite a bit startled, but not at all frightened.

Walt Slade was usually very much at ease in the presence of women, but at the moment he was anything but at ease. He actually stammered. "I — I beg your pardon!" he gulped. "I must have opened the wrong door." He started to beat a hurried retreat, but the girl stayed him with a gesture of her little hand.

"Wait," she said in a low, musical voice. "You must be Mr. Walt Slade who saved my brother's life."

"Yes, I'm Slade," he admitted, "and I'm sorry that —"

"Oh, don't worry about it," she interrupted. "It was a perfectly natural mistake. I've done it myself a couple of times; the knobs are close together. Shut the door, it's drafty. There's no harm been done so far as

I can see. I'll slip on a robe and some slippers and then I want to talk to you," she said. "Sit down, won't you?"

A moment later she was snugged in a robe of some clinging stuff that molded itself nicely to the sweet curves of her figure. She thrust her feet into little beaded moccasins and sat down.

"Now, that's better," she said.

"I'm not so sure," Slade disagreed.

She laughed again. "Perhaps not," she admitted, "but we have to accord some respect to the sacred proprieties, don't we? But I want to thank you for what you did for my brother. Clate and I have always been very close to one another, especially after our mother died."

"I didn't do much," he deprecated.

"Only saved his life," she answered. "And I understand you saved Dad's herd from being stolen and saved an oil well from burning up and perhaps destroying a town. Mr. Slade, do you always go about doing good?"

Walt Slade's eyes were suddenly very serious. "Thank you," he said. "I think that is about the nicest compliment I ever received. I only hope I'll be worthy of it."

"I think you are and always will be," she said gravely. "And I hear you've gone to

113

work for Dad. I'm glad; he needs somebody to help him, with Clate flat on his back and Curly Nevins often barely able to walk because of his rheumatism. But it's late and I won't keep you from your rest; you must have had a hard day. I'll see you again in the morning. I suppose I'm a little late in introducing myself, but I'm Mary Mawson, as doubtless you've already guessed."

In the privacy of his own room, Walt Slade thought, Gosh! she's a regular little doll. Slade was tired, but just the same it took him quite a while to get to sleep.

TEN

He saw her again the next morning at the breakfast table. Old Tom performed the introductions which Slade acknowledged gravely, Mary with something very like a grin tugging at her red lips.

"The poor dear would be shocked if he knew about last night," she whispered as they left the dining room. "I'll have to leave you now and give the cook a hand. Here come the Bradded R boys already; there'll be a big crowd here today for the funeral. Poor old Jess!" she added, her wide eyes suddenly misting. "He was with us when I was a little girl."

■ ■ ■ ■

They buried Jess Rader that afternoon under the whispering pines on the hill, where slept Tom Mawson's wife and others of his relations and workers. Most of the cattlemen of the valley were present and many a curious and interested glance rested on the tall man with the black hair and level gray eyes who stood beside Mary Mawson at the open grave.

Slade was surprised to see Wade Ballard, the Black Gold saloon owner, among those present, but he recalled Curly Nevins saying that Tom Mawson had met him in Proctor and thought pretty well of him. So he thought nothing of it when after the funeral Mawson and Ballard walked away together, conversing earnestly. Ballard appeared to be urging something about which old Tom was dubious.

For a while the Walking M cowboys went about their chores in a subdued manner, but death sudden and sharp is too common an occurrence on the rangeland to leave any lasting impression. Before long things had about gotten back to normal.

The following morning Slade rounded up half a dozen of the hands and told them to get ready to ride and to bring wire nippers with them. He led the way to the first of the fenced waterholes on the south range.

"All right," he told the hands, "cut the wire and get those fences down."

The cowboys stared at him. "But, boss," one protested, "we lost nearly fifty cows around this hole."

"You won't lose any more if you keep an eye on the holes," Slade replied. "Get busy!"

After a look at him the punchers decided it best not to argue. With some grumbling, under their breath, they went to work on the fence. Soon the hole was open to the cattle grazing some distance off. Slade led the way to the next hole. The hands obeyed orders and within an hour all the fences were down.

Slade rolled a cigarette and regarded his men in silence for a moment, then he said, "It's nonsense to think that oil in the water would poison cattle. A heavy flow of uncontrolled gas, yes, but oil, never. In the first place if there was a heavy scum on the water as there is on the creek to the south, the cows wouldn't drink it, and even if they did, it wouldn't hurt them. You haven't found any dead stock around the creek, have you?"

The hands were forced to admit they never had.

"And you never will," Slade said. "These holes were deliberately poisoned with arsenic or strychnine, arsenic most likely. I examined the rocks and there was no frosting of arsenic crystals on them, but I suppose you've had some heavy rains since the holes were fenced? I thought so. Which would cause the water to rise enough to wash away any arsenic riming that might have been left. But no matter how much poison was dumped in the holes the water would purify itself in a few days. There is a constant flow from springs into the holes which would take care of that. Unless the holes are poisoned again, which I consider unlikely, nothing more will happen. But we'll keep a watch on them just in case. Incidentally, I drank some of the water yesterday and didn't get any belly cramps."

The cowboys cursed and glared southward. "Want us to keep this quiet, boss?" a wizened old puncher asked.

Slade considered for a moment. "No," he decided. "If the word is spread around that we've caught on to what was done it may tend to alleviate the danger of further poisoning. Nobody would be likely to come snooping around knowing he'd be taking a chance on eating lead."

"What about that spoiled grass down

toward the creek?" another puncher asked.

"The answer to that I don't know as yet," Slade frankly admitted. "The grass roots are undoubtedly being killed by oil seepage, but how it comes the seepage extends so far beyond the field is a question that right now I'm not prepared to answer. I never heard of anything like it before and I don't understand it."

As he spoke he automatically raised his gaze to the hill crests on the west. Abruptly his eyes narrowed a little. From this particular angle he observed something he had not noticed before; the slope of the rimrock was reversed. The slope of the valley was indubitably from north to south, but the slope of the rimrock was just as definitely from south to north. Slade had a feeling that there was an important significance to the phenomenon, just what he couldn't at the moment determine; it would require some thinking out. He dismissed the problem for the time being and turned his attention to more immediate matters.

"We'll ride east and have a look at the canyons and draws over there," he told his men. "I've a notion those gulches will require considerable combing. The old man figures to run his shipping herd north to the railroad next week and seeing as we have

118

the time he wants to add as many beefs as he can to it. The Bradded R and the Turkey Track up to the north have decided to join with us and have a round-up so they can roll herds, too. The old man wants to get the round-up started tomorrow if possible and it won't hurt for us to look over the ground a bit today while we have the chance. It's logical to believe those gulches will comb to advantage; cows hole up this time of the year."

A careful going-over of the broken ground proved Slade's surmise was correct; there were plenty of fat beefs seeking the coolness and good grass of the canyons.

"We'll have our work cut out for us in these cracks, but it'll pay off," he said. "Well, I guess we'd better be heading for home."

Old Tom's reaction to Slade's account of the poisoned waterholes was explosively profane.

"That was just an act of pure danged cussedness, nothing less," he concluded. "Just somebody trying to start trouble."

"Yes," Slade agreed thoughtfully, "it sure looks like somebody had just that in mind, to start trouble."

"The blasted sidewinders!" growled Mawson. "The devil with them! Let's start figuring that round-up. I'm going to see to it that you are made round-up and trail boss; I want somebody handling the chore I can depend on."

The round-up got under way the following morning. When the other owners appeared on the scene old Tom insisted that Slade be appointed boss of the round-up. The Bradded R and Turkey Track owners, who had met Slade at the funeral of Jess Rader and had already sized him up, offered no objections.

Slade had all the responsibility and was absolutely in control of the round-up, for it is an unwritten law of the rangeland that not even an owner can dispute or question the round-up boss' orders.

His first act was to select his assistants from the cowboys gathered for the work. Each was put in command of a group of riders who would thoroughly scour the range in search of vagrant cattle as well as large bunches.

"I don't want any mavericks when this chore is over," Slade told them. "Mavericks left after a round-up are a sign of careless combing. I want everything out of the canyons and brakes, and I want cows, not excuses."

The hands resolved there would be neither mavericks nor excuses. They didn't hanker to do any explaining to this particular round-up boss.

Slade sent the riders out in troops. Each troop would spread out over the range, dividing into smaller parties which presently scattered until the men were separated by distances that varied according to the topography of the country. Each man had to hunt out all the cattle on the section over which he rode. On the broken ground near the hills and in the canyons careful searching for small clumps or cannily holed-up old mossybacks was necessary.

The cows were gathered up in groups as large as the rider or riders could handle and driven to a designated holding spot where they were held in close herd. After the round-up boss decided a sufficient number had been assembled, the riders mounted fresh horses and the business of cutting out the various brands began. Into the milling, bawling and thoroughly bad-tempered mass went the riders, and it was a difficult and dangerous task. The cows dodged, the horsemen swore and finally the critter in question, mad as a hornet, was shoved to where the cut was being formed. Next the beefs were driven before the tally man who carefully checked off the brands. According to brand, the animals were distributed to the subsidiary holding spots of the various ranches.

Day after day the cowboys toiled in the dust and heat. Group after group of cattle streamed in. The various herds steadily grew larger. Only choice animals were held on this particular beef round-up, the others would be allowed to drift back onto the range.

Slade set his night guards with care. He didn't think anybody would attempt a wide-looping while the herds were at the holding spots, but a foolhardy raid might easily set off a stampede that would scatter the cows, mad with fright, all over the range, which would necessitate doing the work all over.

And while automatically attending to his numerous chores, he was constantly study-ing the bleak hills that soared up on three sides, for he was confident that somewhere in their granite breasts was locked the explanation of the recent weird happenings in the once peaceful valley. One day, near the close of the round-up, he hit on an old trail, little more than a game track, that wound up the fairly gentle side slope of a canyon. To all appearances it led to the rim-rock far above. Acting on a sudden impulse he sent Shadow up the narrow track. An hour later he came out on the rim.

From where he sat his great black horse on the dizzy eminence the view was splendid; the valley and its surrounding hills were spread before his eyes like a map. He studied the green floor so far below him. Yes, the valley slope was definitely from north to south, but the hills were different. To the south they were much higher than to the north. A definite reversal of contours. He envisioned the terrain as it must have been a million, perhaps ten million years before. The whole great basin was a sheet of tossing water. Yellow sand banks extended far into the wide inland sea. Its verge was a mass of tall reeds and stupendous vegetation in which huge monsters, scaled and tailed, wallowed and fought. Farther back was the bold shore line that now formed the hills which encircled the bowl. Even the surface of the shore line was doubtless naked stone, while near the water the monstrous vegetation grew with incredible rapidity, died as swiftly and fell, layer on layer, into the turgid water, sinking to the primal ooze, washed over by silt and sand, sinking deeper and deeper under the accumulated weight, while in the dark depths the slow and subtle chemistry of nature wrought unexplainable change.

Followed a long period of upheaval, when the mountains spouted fire and the waters shook to terrestrial thunderings. Slowly the shore line rose higher, and the bed of the wide sea sank. A mighty convulsion, when the earth writhed in agony, caused the great fault that culminated in the subsidence of a wide area to the south to form what was now the desert. The slope of the sea floor reversed under the volcanic hammerings. The water, deprived of surface flow by the heightening of the hills, shrank to shallow pools and marshy lagoons and vanished altogether. Next came a slow process of weathering down, then more volcanic action. The encircling wall that had been the shore line was rent and shattered. Fissures like the canyon beneath came into being. Streams again flowed into the basin, now much shallower, and cut channels across its surface, made their way down the slope from the cap rock and lost themselves in the sands of the desert or by way of subterranean channels reached the Rio Grande and the sea. And that was how the rangeland that was now Weirton Valley came into being.

Walt Slade pondered all this while he studied the hills. He wondered just how deep the reversal that tilted the valley floor from north to south continued. For upon the possible depth of the reversal depended a nebulous theory that was building up in his mind and might lead to the explanation he sought. Heavy with thought, he rode back down the trail to supervise the final round-up chores.

That evening the various herds were driven to their home pastures where they would be held for a few days until the drive north to the railroad and the shipping pens got under way.

"Best handled round-up I ever had anything to do with," declared old Tom Mawson. The other owners nodded sober agreement.

The following afternoon Slade rode to Weirton, feeling that he should keep an eye on the activities of the oil town. He did not follow the Chihuahua but rode directly south to the creek before turning west, desiring to study its environs a bit more. Upon reaching the ford he splashed his horse through the water and entered the town. He found Bob Kent busy around his workings. The oilman paused in his activities to greet Slade and have a talk.

"That darn Blaine Richardson has got me bothered," he confessed. "Yesterday he rode down to the desert with two of his best drillers and a pack mule. He came back toward evening but he didn't bring the drillers or the mule with him. Looks like he's establishing a permanent camp down there. I wonder if he has got the right notion and that down there was the real inland sea and the best deposit. I'm half of the notion to buy a hunk of that land from the state on the chance that he might be right."

Slade shot the oilman an exasperated glance. "Kent," he said, "even a limited knowledge of geology should tell you that the desert was never part of the inland sea."

"But that engineer from the Spindletop field said it was," Kent protested.

"If he did, he lied," Slade replied shortly. "No certificated engineer would make such a mistake. The desert was at one time but a continuation of the hills to the east and west, part of the shoreline of the sea that covered what is now Weirton Valley. The desert came into being in the course of the subsidence that created the Balcones Fault. It was never under water, at least at no period that is covered by geological and petrological survey, and the period of scientific survey covers the formation of oil pools."

Kent looked a little blank, but convinced.

"And then you'd say there is no oil under the desert?"

"I would hesitate to make such a dogmatic statement," Slade replied. "We must take into consideration the fact that we do not know what occurs or has occurred in the depths of the earth. Through overflow or seepage there might possibly be some oil under the desert, although I consider it highly improbable. But even if there is, it would be but a shallow deposit that would not compare with what you have up here. My advice to you is to leave the desert alone and not waste your money acquiring title to any of it." He paused, and then let the full force of his level eyes rest on the oilman's face. "And Kent," he added, "I want you to keep what I've just told you under your hat. Don't talk to anybody about it. If it becomes common knowledge that you've learned what you did today, you may come up missing some dark night."

Kent looked decidedly startled. "What the devil do you mean?" he asked.

"I mean," Slade told him, "that there's something very strange going on in this section. Just what it is I don't know, but I'm convinced that whoever is back of it will stop at nothing including murder to keep from being thwarted in whatever they have in mind. And I have a feeling that Blaine Richardson's activities down on the desert in some way ties up with the business."

Bob Kent shook his head in a bewildered fashion. "I can hardly follow just what the devil you're talking about," he admitted, "but dang it, you've got me scared."

"Stay scared and the chances are you'll last longer," Slade advised. "Right now I don't believe you are in any personal danger, but a few careless words reaching the wrong pair of ears may mark you for elimination. Don't forget it."

"I won't," Kent promised. "From now on I ain't even going to talk in my sleep."

"A good notion," Slade chuckled.

"But what about you?" Kent asked.

"Oh, I hope nobody hereabouts is aware of what I know," Slade replied cheerfully. "Don't see any reason why they should be."

Kent shook his head again. "You're a funny feller for a wandering cowpoke," he said.

"Perhaps, for a wandering cowpoke," Slade agreed with a smile.

But despite what he said to Kent, Walt Slade knew well that he himself was marked for death and did not relax his vigilance.

A little later he headed back for the Walking M, riding the Chihuahua Trail that edged closer and closer to the hill slopes as it trended north.

Slade continuously studied those wooded slopes, carefully noting the movements of birds and the little animals that scuttled through the growth. Abruptly his attention centered on a bristle of growth a little ways up the slope past which he was riding. Over the thicket several birds were wheeling and fluttering and uttering sharp cries. What had disturbed them, he wondered.

His eyes dropped to the dark clump of growth where each outer branch and twig shimmered in the sunlight. Even as a spurt of whitish smoke wisped from the brush he was going sideways from the saddle. He struck the ground on the far side of his horse and lay motionless just beyond the outer edge of the trail, half hidden by the short grass. The hard, metallic clang of a rifle shot slammed back and forth among the cliffs.

Shadow trotted on a few paces, then paused to glance back inquiringly at his master's huddled form.

ELEVEN

For long minutes nothing happened. Slade still lay sprawled in the grass. The birds that had flown higher at the sound of the shot were again swooping and crying over the topmost branches. Otherwise the thicket was devoid of sound or motion.

Then abruptly there was movement in the growth. The branches parted and a horseman rode cautiously into view; he was followed by another. Slowly, bending low in their saddles, rifle barrels jutting forward, the drygulchers descended the slope. They could just make out the body of their victim lying motionless beside the trail.

What they hadn't seen was Slade drag his Winchester from the saddle boot as he fell. Now he lay with his cheek cuddled against the stock, his eyes glancing along the sights.

On came the drygulchers, walking their horses. They relaxed a little. One turned his head to speak to the other. Slade lay utterly motionless.

Nearer and nearer drew the slowly pacing horses. Slade counted off the distance — three hundred yards, two hundred and fifty, two hundred. His finger tightened on the trigger. And abruptly one of the killers sensed that something was not just right. He straightened in his saddle, clamped his rifle butt to his shoulder. Slade pulled trigger.

The report of the heavy rifle rang out like

thunder in the stillness and before the echoes slammed back, the foremost drygulcher threw up his hands and pitched headlong. His companion yelled with fright and fired wildly, the bullet hissing over Slade's body.

A second time the Winchester spoke. Two riderless horses galloped off a little ways and paused snorting and blowing, staring back with rolling eyes at the two sprawled shapes on the ground.

For long minutes Slade lay motionless, his glance shifting from the bodies of the drygulchers to the thicket above. He saw the irritated birds settle into the growth. They did not rise again and he cautiously got to his feet. Cocked rifle ready for instant action he climbed the slope to where the two bodies lay; as he neared them he lowered the hammer of the rifle. He had gotten both the fanging sidewinders dead center. But he knew well that if he hadn't noticed the way the disturbed birds were acting up and seen the sunlight glint on the rifle barrel as it was shifted to line sights, he would have gotten it dead center.

The two drygulchers were hard looking specimens, even in death. One had a vaguely familiar look but Slade could not place him at the moment. Their pockets discovered

nothing of significance, they wore regula-
tion rangeland garb, each packed a heavy
sixshooter in addition to the rifles lying
nearby. The rigs on the horses were ordinary
and the animals bore meaningless Mexican
skillet-of-snakes brands.

Suddenly Slade jumped a foot as a rau-
cous bray burst from the thicket above. He
whirled about, gun in hand, but the thicket
produced nothing more. With a last look
around he scrambled up the slope, pushed
the growth aside and found himself in a
small grass grown clearing that was hidden
from the trail below. A tiny spring bubbled
from under a rock and beside the spring
were the ashes of a fire, some tumbled
blankets, a bucket and a skillet and a store
of staple provisions. Nearby a haltered mule
surveyed him amiably.

Slade stared at the mule and abruptly
recalled Bob Kent's remark that Blaine
Richardson and his two drillers had a pack
mule with them when they headed for the
desert the day before and that Richardson
returned minus the drillers and the mule.
He wondered could this possibly be the
same mule, and were the dead men farther
down the slope the drillers in question. He
hadn't forgotten that it was one of Richardson's hands, Nate Persinger, who had

endeavored to kill him in the Black Gold saloon. Began to look like an interesting bit of coincidence, to say the least.

The significance of the mule and the provisions was now plainly apparent. The drygulchers had made a camp here in the thicket and preparations to hole up for quite a while if necessary. Doubtless they had reasoned that sooner or later he would be riding to town and had planned their campaign of murder accordingly.

"And if I'd happened to have ridden the Chihuahua this morning instead of over to the east, I'd have very likely gotten it," he muttered. "Patient and persevering sidewinders! But maybe somebody slipped a little this time; we'll try and find out."

He loosed the mule and led the docile creature down to the trail. He had no trouble catching the two well-trained horses that were cropping grass nearby. Before securing the bodies to the saddles he examined the dead men's pockets with care and was rather surprised to find no trace of oily grit in the linings. Doubtless, however, the pair had changed clothes before starting on their drygulching expedition. Mounting Shadow and leading the burdened horses and the mule he headed back to town.

A crowd quickly gathered, following at a

discreet distance, as the grisly procession clicked down the main street of Weirton. Just as Slade reached Deputy Hawkins' office, Bob Kent came running up, volleying questions. The deputy, aroused by the tumult, stepped from the office to add his queries to the oilman's.

"Tell you about it later," Slade returned briefly. He unloaded the bodies and placed them on the ground.

"Ever see these jiggers before, Bob?" he asked expectantly.

Kent looked blank and shook his head. "Never did, so far as I can recall," he replied.

Slade's eyes narrowed a little; his lips tightened. It appeared his nicely built up theory was neatly scrambled.

Deputy Hawkins was peering at the dead faces. "I've seen this short one before," he exclaimed. "He used to ride in from somewhere every now and then and loaf around the saloons. Never seemed to have anything to do but always had plenty of money to spend. I didn't like his looks and kept an eye on him, but he always behaved himself. Don't think I ever talked with him."

Slade nodded but did not otherwise comment.

"Won't you please tell us what this is all

about?" the deputy begged.

Slade told them, in terse sentences. Hawkins swore with feeling as the tale progressed.

"The snake-blooded hellions!" he stormed. "They were out to even for that widelooping chore you busted up for them, eh? You did a good chore, Slade, a dang good chore. Wish you'd done for a dozen like them. We'll hold an inquest tomorrow. Drop around if you're a mind to, but don't go to any extra trouble. The law can stretch a point where such scum is being set on; there won't be any trouble about a verdict."

Slade had one more card to play. "Bob," he said to the oilman, "you should know where the livery stables are located. I'd like to try and get the lowdown on this mule. The horses don't mean anything, but the mule might."

"Sure I know where they are, there are only three," Kent replied. "Come along, I'll show you."

The first stable they visited was barren of results, the keeper hadn't stalled a mule in a month, but at the second the owner wrinkled his brows as he inspected the long-eared animal.

"Mules all look alike," he said, "but I've a notion I've had that critter here. I think it is the one brought in by a couple of fellers day before yesterday, a tall feller and a short one. They put it up with their horses and yesterday they took it out again. Nope, I don't know where they went with it; I didn't pay any attention to them after they left."

"Well, put it up again and keep it till Deputy Hawkins calls for it," Slade told him.

"And that's that," he remarked to Kent as they left the stable. "Let's go get something to eat."

From force of habit, Kent led the way to the Black Gold. The news of the drygulching had evidently gotten around and Slade was the target for many stares when they entered the saloon. Wade Ballard came over to the table, smiling as usual.

"Well, Slade, you seem to have been seeing plenty of action since you coiled your twine here," he observed. "And now it would appear you are the recipient of attention from the outlaw fraternity. I'd say you're able to hold your own, but don't underestimate 'em; those hellions are bad, plumb cultus. You'll do well to keep your eyes skun. I'll send over drinks."

"Wade is quite a feller," Bob Kent remarked.

"An unusual character," Slade replied as his eyes followed the saloonkeeper across the room.

After eating, Slade resumed his interrupted ride to the Walking M ranchhouse in no very affable frame of mind. What had appeared to be a promising lead had petered out. Either his conclusions had been erroneous or he had been nicely outsmarted; he wasn't sure which. If Richardson or someone of his outfit had engineered the deal, they had covered up beautifully. Doubtless right now the two drillers were down by the well Richardson was sinking in the desert. Perhaps the mule was the same Bob Kent saw the drillers leading out of town, but then again perhaps it wasn't. And if it was, the drillers could have later delivered the provision laden animal to the drygulchers. He wished that he had thought to ask Kent to describe the two drillers. One of them might have been tall, the other short. All conjecture, of course, but it appeared that at the moment conjecture was about all he had to go on.

Of course Deputy Hawkins might be right in his surmise that the drygulching was in retaliation for his frustration of the wide-looping. But Slade didn't think so. It had displayed the same careful planning that characterized the attempt on his life in the Black Gold. The similarity of pattern was a bit too striking to write off as just coincidence.

What puzzled Slade most was the apparent anomaly that was Blaine Richardson. Unless his estimate of the man was surprisingly inaccurate, Richardson was just not the type to originate and put into practice such subtle and devious schemes. Slade felt that his methods would be much more likely to parallel those he attributed to old Tom Mawson: they would be direct and in line with the man's undoubted impulsiveness. He began to wonder if Richardson might be much more crafty than showed on the surface.

Wade Ballard also puzzled Slade more than a little. Ballard appeared to make a studied effort to pass as a rough, almost uncouth westerner of little education or culture. But in moments of abstraction his use of words was a bit surprising. Slade hadn't forgotten his comment at the burning well: ". . . and the corollary is that the fire could be extinguished with an arrow."

The use of the words corollary and extinguished appeared definitely at variance with the character the man assumed. Slade was developing an uneasy feeling that Ballard might well be mixed up in the baffling affair in one way or another. But how, where or why he had not the slightest notion.

He had also not forgotten that it was Ballard, according to Bob Kent's version of the matter, who had relayed to the oilman the agreement of the engineer from the Spindletop oil field with Richardson's theory that the desert had once been the real bed of the inland sea. Either the engineer, if he was an engineer as he claimed to be, had deliberately lied, or Ballard had passed on to Kent a perverted version of what he had said. Slade swore wearily and settled himself in the saddle for the long ride home.

TWELVE

The shipping herd got underway on schedule. "The Turkey Track leads the way," Tom Mawson told Slade. "Then comes Tol Releford's Bradded R, and we bring up the rear. We figure to hold them about a quarter mile apart and we use separate bedding grounds to keep the danged critters from mixing up. Plenty of good spots and always water. Horse Creek runs close to the trail almost the whole way."

No one rode immediately in front of the marching cattle, but off to the side and near the head rode the point men whose duty it was to veer the herd when a change of direction was desired. To this chore Slade assigned four men, two on each side. This was double the usual number assigned to the chore, but Slade was taking no chances. They paced their horses about a third of the way back from the head of the column. Another third of the way back rode the swing men, where the column would begin to bend in case of a change of direction. These were also doubled. Still another third of the way back were flank riders. These assisted the swing riders in blocking any tendency on the part of the cows to sideways wandering, and in driving off any foreign cattle that might seek to join the herd. A triple force of drag riders brought up the rear, swearing at the dust, the heat and the stragglers. Next came the remuda of spare horses in charge of a wrangler and the lumbering chuck wagon driven by the cook. As an added precaution against a possible raid, Slade had outriders fanning out from the herd and inspecting the country ahead.

Usually the trail boss rides far ahead to survey the ground and search out watering-places and good grazing grounds for the bedding down at night, but under the circumstances with the bedding grounds decided on in advance, this was not necessary and Slade mostly rode drag with the main body of his men. At times, however, he rode along the herd or even detoured to get in front of the column and study the terrain over which they had to pass.

The first day Slade shoved the herd along fast to get them off their home range where they evinced greater tendency to stray and covered a full twenty-five miles of distance. After the first day he reduced the speed to half, for to push the cattle too fast would mean to run valuable fat and weight off them. He figured on three days to cover the remaining slightly more than forty miles to McCarney.

Until the trail entered the hills north of the valley the going was good. Then the drive became slow and hard with steep slopes to breast and narrow stretches where the herd was strung out in almost single file with rugged slopes flinging up to the right and left.

Late afternoon of the third day they reached a point where the trail forked. Before starting the drive the owners had decided to take the left fork through Hanging Rock Canyon instead of the longer route by way of Horsehead Canyon.

"We'll cut off nearly ten miles of driving that way," Mawson explained to Slade. "We can't use the short cut in wet weather or

141

during the spring thaws. Hanging Rock is too danged dangerous then. Boulders come tumbling down, sometimes whole bunches of them, but this time of the year she's safe enough even though she don't look it."

Early morning of the fourth day out the herd got underway with the expectancy of reaching McCarney before sunset. At the moment the trail wound through thick brush growing on either side at no great distance from the track and curtailing the view ahead. They had covered less than a mile when a tumult broke loose up front. The point men were shouting, the swing riders yelling questions. Slade and Mawson raced their horses along the moving column of cattle to find out what was going on. They reached a point near the head of the column where the brush fell away to form a clearing of some acres in extent, across which meandered a small stream.

The clearing was dotted with cattle charging back and forth in every direction, with cursing riders working like blazes to round them up and get them into herd. Near the trail stood a well blistered and still smoking chuck wagon, around which stamped a squat and corpulent gentleman who raised both clenched fists to the heavens and spouted appalling profanity. Slade recognized him as Tol Releford, the Bradded R owner.

"Tol, what in blazes happened?" shouted old Tom as they pulled up beside him.

Releford shook his fist at a lanky, elderly individual with a limp who was industriously dousing stray sparks with water.

"He did it!" he bellowed. "All cooks are crazy, but that frazzled end of a misspent life is the prime specimen of the lot!"

"Shut up, you hammered down hunk of tallow!" the limper squalled reply. "How the devil did I know the dang thing would do it? When I get back to Proctor I'm goin' to shoot Bige Bixley for selling it to me!"

"Tol," Mawson pleaded, "won't you tell us what the devil's the meaning of all this?"

Releford again shook his fist at the cook. "That spavined old pelican!" he sputtered. "He goes and buys one of those infernal new-fangled oil stoves to keep in the chuck wagon and warm up his rheumatism. This morning right after breakfast the dang thing blew up. Sounded like the sky was falling. It set fire to the chuck wagon and the canvas top shot flames into the air a couple of hundred feet. Scared the tails off the cows and they stampeded in every direction. They couldn't run far, thank Pete, but they sure scattered to the devil and gone. Go ahead with your herd, Tom, we'll be right on your heels soon as we straighten out this mess."

Shaking with laughter, Slade and Mawson rode on after their cows, leaving the irate Releford and the equally irate cook to settle their differences as best they could.

"Things like that have been going on between those two for the past forty years," chuckled Mawson. "Tol's a bachelor and so is Stiffy Cole, the cook. They love each other like brothers and they're all the time fighting. Tol's quite a hombre. His spread is one of the smallest in this section, but I've a notion he's about as well heeled as anybody hereabouts. Reckon it wouldn't make much difference to him if he never sold another cow, but he likes to keep moving."

It was shortly before noon of the fourth day that the herd reached Hanging Rock Canyon.

"There she is," said Mawson, gesturing to the mouth of the narrow gorge ahead. A few minutes later Slade let out a whistle.

"Good Lord! what a hole!" he exclaimed.

The trail, which was not very wide, necessitating the cattle stringing out in a long line, followed a bench that clung to the west wall of the canyon. From the bench a steep slope tumbled down to the floor of the canyon proper, through which ran a thread of water. On the east it was walled by beetling cliffs.

To the west the vista was appallingly different. It was a mighty slope absolutely destitute of growth, a gray, drab, million-faceted ascent of rocks, a mountain-side wearing down, weathering away, cracked into a myriad of pieces, every one of which had both smooth and sharp surfaces. It had the criss-cross appearance of a net of rock, numberless stones of numberless shapes pieced together by some colossal hand and now split and broken and ready to fall. Frost and heat and the beat of wind and rain had disintegrated the mountain-side till it hung in almost perpendicular splintered ruin, the heaps of broken stone clinging there as if by magic, every one of the endless heaps leaning ready to roll. From the innumerable facets the sun flashed back as from countless mirrors.

Slade glanced down at the canyon floor below. It was littered with talus, studded with boulders and fragments, some of them weighing tons. And above the slope towered dark and terrible and forbidding.

"See why it ain't safe to go through here during wet weather or the thaws?" remarked old Tom as with the cowboys all bunched behind the drag they entered the canyon.

145

"Them rocks are all the time tumbling down."

"And some day the whole dang mess will slide down," Slade predicted. "It's a wonder it hasn't done it before now."

"Maybe," conceded Mawson, "but it's been like this ever since I can remember, and that goes back to close onto fifty years."

The trail had a gentle upward slope to a crest at the north mouth of the gorge which was not very long, hardly more than a mile. The lead cows dipped over, the others followed. The drag reached the crest and the cowboys raced down the opposite sag where the country opened up to take their places along the marching column. Slade paused on the summit and gazed back at the frightful slope hanging poised over the trail. A few minutes later he saw the van of the Bradded R herd enter the canyon, then the hands riding bunched behind the moving cattle that trudged along stolidly under the upward sweeping wave of shattered stone. Slade's eyes travelled up the flashing, concave surface.

From the rimrock, more than a thousand feet above, suddenly mushroomed a cloud of yellowish smoke. An instant later to Slade's ears came a muffled boom. A huge section of the rimrock cliff leaned forward, slowly at first, then with swiftly accelerated speed. The mountain trembled to the crash of its fall.

Instantly the whole slope seemed to be in motion. Slade was deafened by a thundering roar that rolled and spread, a lifting and throwing of measureless sound punctuated by rattling crashes that boomed and echoed from battlement to battlement. A mighty cloud of dust boiled upward, thinning the sunlight, casting eerie shadows.

Under the billowing pall, Slade saw the Bradded R cowboys wheel their horses and flee madly with death bellowing at their heels. Rushing boulders struck the trail around, behind and in front of them and bounded off into the canyon depths, lending wings to the hoofs of the terrified horses. His palms sweating, his face rigid with strain, Slade saw them reach the distant canyon mouth and vanish.

So absorbed had he been in the cowhands' race with death he had hardly noticed what happened to the doomed cattle, now buried beneath countless tons of stone.

The canyon was a seething caldron of dust through which the falling rocks boomed and screamed and rumbled. It billowed upward in fantastic shapes that seemed to toss and writhe in torment, shuddering to the loudening concussion of the avalanche, hiding the horror of the depths.

Back up the slope sped the Walking M hands. They jerked their horses to a halt beside Slade, their eyes wild and staring.

"What the devil happened?" panted old Tom. "Did the danged thing come down at last?"

"Looks sort of that way," Slade replied.

"Good God!" muttered Mawson. "And we just got through!"

"Yes, we got through," Slade said slowly, "but the Bradded R herd didn't. It was in there when the infernal thing cut loose."

"And the boys?" gulped Mawson.

"I think they all got in the clear," Slade reassured him. "It looked that way from up here."

Gradually the mighty voice of the avalanche thinned and deadened, until the silence was broken only by the occasional ringing crack of a belated boulder bounding down the slope. The dust cloud slowly settled and dissipated, revealing the denuded slope and the canyon choked with debris; the trail had vanished.

At the far mouth of the gorge appeared dark blobs that were the Bradded R riders. Slade waved his hand to them and they waved back.

"Well," he said, "I reckon we might as well be shoving along. We can't get to them over that mess. Looks like you won't be able to use this crack as a short cut again. But I expect the railroad will be down your way before you need it again."

"I hope so," Mawson returned gloomily. "I've sure had enough of these infernal hills."

As they rode down the slope Mawson suddenly turned to Slade. His face wore a strained look. "Walt," he said, a bit thickly, "it would have been our herd down under those rocks."

"Yes, very likely it could," Slade admitted.

"And if that had happened, right now I'd be close to being a ruined man," the ranchowner said heavily.

"Guess that was the general notion," Slade replied, and didn't explain just how he meant it. "But it didn't happen," he added cheerfully, "and we should reach McCarney okay in a few hours."

Mawson nodded and was silent.

Walt Slade also rode in silence, for he was thinking deeply. He knew perfectly well that what he had seen and heard was a dynamite explosion set off for the express purpose of bringing down the avalanche. And there was no doubt in his mind but that it had been timed to cut loose to coincide with the entrance of the last herd into the canyon — Tom Mawson's herd. The dynamiters, more than a thousand feet above, would not have been able to tell that the second herd through the gorge was the Walking M and not the Bradded R. They had followed instructions in line with some preconceived plan and only a freak happening had saved Mawson's cattle. An act of wanton destruction, nothing less, with the incident of possible mass murder callously disregarded.

But why? Slade didn't have the answer, yet, but his hazy theory regarding what was back of the strange happenings in Weirton Valley was beginning to crystallize.

Without further untoward occurrence they reached McCarney and the railroad a couple of hours before sundown. The cattle were immediately shunted into the loading pens and old Tom heaved a deep sigh of relief when a stock car door closed on the last cow.

Shortly after the chore was finished, the Bradded R bunch raced their reeking horses into town, having taken the long detour by way of Horsehead Canyon.

That night the Walking M and Turkey Track hands celebrated the safe arrival of their herds in McCarney. The Bradded R punchers didn't have much to celebrate aside from their escape from the avalanche, but they did their manful best to make the occasion a success. It was, to which aching heads and bleary eyes attested the following morning when the long ride back to Weirton Valley started. Walt Slade and the ranch-owners celebrated with greater moderation and were in somewhat better shape.

Old Tom was still puzzling over what started the avalanche. "Reckon it must have been the vibrations set up by our cows passing along the trail," he hazarded, "but I never heard tell of anything like it before. A thousand herds have gone through that crack and nothing happened."

Walt Slade arrived at a decision. "Mr. Mawson," he said, "I'm going to tell you something, but I want you to keep it under your hat."

"I will, whatever it was," promised the rancher. "Shoot! What you got to tell me?"

"That the avalanche was not set off by the vibrations created by the passing herd," Slade replied. "It was deliberately set off by a dynamite explosion on the rimrock. I heard and saw it."

Old Tom stared at him in bewilderment. "But what the devil!" he exploded. "Why in tarnation would anybody do a thing like that? What did they have in mind?"

"In my opinion, what they had in mind was to ruin you financially if possible," Slade answered grimly.

Mawson grew even more bewildered. "You mean those danged oilmen?" he sputtered.

"Definitely not," Slade told him. "I'm willing to wager that as a whole the oil operators and their employees are too busy with their own affairs to give you more than a passing thought. To think that they poisoned your waterholes and tried to destroy your shipping herd is as ridiculous as their accusing you and your hands of setting fire to their wells. Even more so, in fact. It might be maintained that you have a grievance against them because of your spoiled pastures, while their assumption that the cattlemen fired their wells is mere conjecture, as they would be forced to admit."

"Then who the devil did blow those rocks down?" Mawson demanded.

"I haven't the answer, but I hope eventually to have it, possibly with your help," Slade told him.

"You'll get any I can give you, though I don't know what the devil it could be," Mawson growled. "Poisoning waterholes and burying cows under rocks! Why that's

152

worse than murder!"

"I can hardly agree with you there," Slade smiled, adding without a smile, "but if the Bradded R riders had been just a little farther up the canyon when the blast was set off, it would have been murder."

"You're right about that," Mawson agreed. "The snake-blooded hellions!" He eyed his range boss curiously and repeated Bob Kent's remark, "Walt, you're a funny feller for a wandering cowpoke," he said.

"Possibly," Slade replied with another smile, "for a wandering cowpoke."

Thirteen

Mawson was still a bit dubious about the waterholes on the south pasture, so the next day he and Slade rode down to give the holes a once-over. They found cattle grazing contentedly in the vicinity and there were no casualties.

"I don't think they'll try it again," Slade said, "but just the same I have one of the boys scouting around here every night so as not to take any chances."

"But why the devil did they do it in the first place?" Mawson wanted to know. "All they could do was knock off a few head of stock, not enough to do any real damage."

153

"To heighten the tension between the ranchers and the oilmen," Slade replied. "It's an old outlaw trick, sir; set two outfits on the prod against each other, then each blames the other for anything that happens. Which makes a nice cover-up for smooth and salty gents operating in the section. Remember the old fable about the two families of ducks that were fighting over which should have the eel head they'd found? Well, while they were busy fighting one another, along came a cat and carried off the eel head."

Old Tom tugged his mustache and 'lowed it sort of made sense.

They rode on south and paused on the edge of the wide area of withered grass. Mawson scowled at his ruined pastures and rumbled oaths. "No doubt as to what did that, though," he growled. "The cussed oil is responsible for that and there's no getting away from it."

"Yes, the oil is responsible for that," Slade conceded, his eyes thoughtful. As had become a habit with him, he raised his gaze to the rugged hill crests.

"And it's sure raised the devil," Mawson continued. "All this section no good for cows any more. I've a notion to take Wade Ballard up on his offer to buy it."

Slade's glance dropped quickly to the rancher's face. "How's that?" he asked. "You say Ballard wants to buy down here?"

"That's right," Mawson replied. "He made me an offer when he was at the ranchhouse for Jess Rader's burying."

"What reason did he give for wanting to buy?" Slade asked.

"Oh, he was open and above board with his reason, all right," Mawson answered. "He said it's just about sure for certain that the railroad is coming down this way and that they'll plan to build shops and supply stores and a big assembling yard here, or so he figures. He says if that happens it will be a good section to open up a couple more saloons and other places of entertainment and he'd like to get in on the ground floor. He pointed out that if the railroad really wanted and needed the land, they could invoke Eminent Domain and force me to sell to them even if I didn't want to. Reckon he has something there, all right."

"And what did you tell him?" Slade asked curiously.

"I told him I'd think it over," Mawson replied. "He said he knew that of course I wouldn't want to sell just a little chunk down here so he made me an offer for the whole strip this side of the creek. A pretty good offer, too, conditions being what they are, and I reckon I'm a fool not to take him up on it. But somehow I hate to let go of any of my holding; sort of a sentimental reason or some such foolishness, I reckon. I was born and brought up on the Walking M and it's got to be a part of me, as it were. If I'd lost the shipping herd the other day, I reckon I wouldn't have had much choice in the matter if I wanted to stay in business. I'd been forced to scrape up money somewhere to meet that bank payment, but because you saved my herd from those thieving hellions and then got it and the other five hundred head safe to the pens, things ain't quite so tight as they were. What do you think about it, Walt?"

"I think," Slade replied slowly, "that while Ballard is right about the railroad building down this way — I heard in McCarney that they're already rushing plans for construction — he is mistaken when he figures they'll build shops and a yard down here. The C. & P. already have extensive repair shops, supply depots and a large assembling yard at McCarney, so why should they duplicate down here? If they choose this valley for their route to Mexico, their next great division point will be south of the Rio Grande for sound business reasons, to promote good feeling, stimulate trade from the south, and so forth. If they just build a spur to tap the oil transportation from here, all they'll need is a turntable and a few side tracks. Understand, sir?"

"Yes, I think I do," Mawson nodded. "I'd never thought of it in that light. So it would appear to be good business to unload a worthless holding on Ballard, eh?"

"Are you asking my advice, sir?" Slade countered.

"Yes, I am," Mawson stated definitely.

Slade's answer was obliquely in the form of a question. "Ever play a hunch?" he asked.

"Yep," old Tom chuckled. "I've filled an inside straight more than once on a hunch."

"Well," Slade smiled, "right now I'm playing a hunch, a hunch that if you sell to Ballard, no matter what he offers, that you will be disposing of an immensely valuable property for a mere fraction of its worth. I have as yet nothing that could be called definite on which to base my hunch, but it's working mighty strong, and I hope to before long have something that will solidly foundation it. So if you are willing to take the chance of filling another inside straight, my advice is not to sell."

Old Tom chuckled again. "Son," he said,

"I've a notion if you really set your head to it, you could talk a sidewinder out of fangin'. I'd just about decided to take Ballard up on his offer, but now I won't, at least not yet. I'll give you a chance to play your hunch, whatever it is. After all, if things don't seem to work out right I can always reconsider and if Ballard figures he's right about the railroad building here, I've a notion his offer will stand."

"Yes, I think you can rely on its standing," Slade replied, a trifle grimly. "And now suppose we ride down to Weirton for a drink and a bite to eat?"

Old Tom stared. "To that stinkin' hole!" he exploded.

"Yes, and I've a notion you'll decide it doesn't smell as bad as you think it does," Slade replied with a grin. "Fact is, I think it's a real good notion."

Mawson threw out his hands in a resigned gesture. "What I said about the sidewinder goes for a whole nest of 'em," he declared. "Oh, all right, only I hope I don't get pizened!"

Walt Slade rode south in a complacent frame of mind. What had formerly been but hazy supposition was now concrete. The act of seemingly malicious mischief in Hanging Rock Canyon had achieved definite purpose. He at last had pinned down the elusive motive. Wade Ballard and perhaps others associated with him, doubtless including Blaine Richardson, wanted Tom Mawson's land and were prepared to go to any lengths to acquire it.

Why? The answer to that was fairly obvious, but the reasoning upon which Ballard evidently based his conclusions was not so obvious. Slade knew that the experienced oilmen were convinced that the only oil in Weirton Valley was under the mesa south of the creek. As Arch Caldwell pointed out, if the deposit extended north of the creek for any appreciable distance, with the slope of the valley definitely from north to south, the pressure would be much greater. Bob Kent's initial gusher would have continued to gush for an extended period. The speedy easing of the pressure, Caldwell and others maintained, was due to the fact that the pool, comparatively speaking, a small one, was concentrated under the mesa. If Ballard believed there was oil under Mawson's land, his opinion was certainly at variance with that held by men who should know what they were talking about, apparently as senseless, indeed, as the dry hole Blaine Richardson was drilling out on the desert.

Walt Slade had his own theory, based on

a much more than average knowledge of geological phenomena and an exhaustive study of the contours of the terrain, but he was forced to admit that it was only a theory that could be proven or disproven only by a very expensive test. He wondered if he could talk Mawson and Bob Kent into making the test with no guarantee of positive results.

He wondered, too, if Ballard had hit on the same idea. It was not beyond the realm of possibility. He felt assured that Wade Ballard was something quite different from what he professed to be and wished he had time to dig into his past a bit and learn something of his background. That, at the moment, however, was out of the question.

Meanwhile, his primary chore was to try and drop a loop on whoever it was responsible for the depredations committed in Weirton Valley, which loomed as considerable of a chore. For no matter what he might think, at present he had not one iota of proof against anybody.

The Black Gold was used to sensations of one sort or another, but when Slade and Tom Mawson walked in and sat down at a table, the stares were almost audible.

Old Tom glared about suspiciously, sniffing for all the world like an animal that scents danger. Slade stifled a grin and ordered drinks.

"Excuse me a minute, sir," he said to the rancher. "I see a fellow at the bar I want to speak to."

He walked to the bar and accosted old Arch Caldwell who greeted him warmly. A moment later from the tail of his eye he saw Wade Ballard saunter across the room and sit down opposite Mawson. They talked together earnestly for several minutes, then Ballard got up and returned to the end of the bar. And for once he wasn't smiling and there was a hard glitter in the depths of his clear eyes.

"Come over and say hello to Mr. Mawson," Slade suggested to Caldwell. "I've a notion you'll like him."

"Scared I won't be welcome," Caldwell hesitated.

"We'll risk it," Slade replied cheerfully. "Come along."

He led the oilman to the table and performed the introductions. Old Tom grunted acknowledgment gruffly, but didn't look as gruff as he sounded. Caldwell sat down diffidently. Slade ordered another round of drinks and gradually edged out of the conversation.

It developed that Caldwell had once been

in the cattle business and that his two sons still were. He and Mawson began discussing range matters, cautiously at first, but with increasing animation. A few minutes later Slade left the table and returned to the bar to greet Bob Kent who had just entered. And when he went back to the table he took Kent with him.

"Guess you know Bob, Mr. Mawson," he remarked as they sat down.

"Sure I know him!" Mawson admitted, sounding gruff again and again not looking as gruff as he sounded. "He's the young squirt responsible for all my troubles. He started it!"

Slade winked at Kent and they began talking to one another, leaving the two oldsters to their discussion of the cattle business.

As they rode home under the stars, old Tom suddenly remarked to Slade, "That Caldwell 'pears to be considerable of a feller when you get to know him."

"Yes, I think he is," Slade replied. "And I think that applies to most people, when we get to know them we learn they're not much different from ourselves."

Old Tom regarded him curiously. "Walt," he said, "in years you're just a young feller, but sometimes I get the feeling that you've lived longer than I have."

"Perhaps I have lived more," Walt Slade answered.

Meanwhile there was a stormy session in the back room of Wade Ballard's saloon. The doors were locked, the shutters closed. Blaine Richardson, scowling and muttering under his breath, paced the floor with jerky steps. Ballard, seated at a table and smoking a cigarette, appeared to find Richardson's gyrations amusing. Half a dozen hard-looking individuals seated at the table with him appeared to find nothing amusing.

"So it would seem you bungled things again," Ballard observed to the glowering Richardson.

"How the devil could I figure out that a danged cook's stove would blow up?" Richardson countered angrily. "Everything was planned right and handled right."

"Except that Mawson's herd wasn't in the canyon," Ballard commented. "I can't understand why you didn't keep a careful check on his movements and learn in time that his herd had switched places with Releford's."

"It never did that before that I've heard tell of," growled Richardson.

"And the rocks in that canyon never fell

before, either," Ballard replied. "Anyhow, the job was bungled and we've got another defeat chalked up against us. Now Mawson isn't as nearly hard pressed for ready cash as he was. I just about had him agreeing to sell, but tonight he'd changed his mind and just said he'd consider it maybe some time later. Yes, he either changed his mind or somebody changed it for him; I'm wondering a bit about that."

"It was that danged wandering cowboy, Walt Slade," declared Richardson. "Things have gone wrong ever since he squatted in this section. He's got to be got rid of."

"You had a couple of tries at it and didn't have much luck," Ballard observed pointedly.

"Things just didn't work out right," Richardson replied defensively. "Next time I'll handle it myself. I might manage to pick a row with him and —"

"And die," Ballard interrupted. "He'd kill you before you cleared leather. And now, friend Richardson, I'm going to tell you something that may really put you on your toes. I recognized him the first time I saw him, that's why I immediately planned to get rid of him. That blamed wandering cowboy, as you call him, is El Halcon."

Richardson abruptly ceased his pacing.

164

He stared at Ballard, his mouth open. The men at the table sat bolt upright.

"You — you sure about that, Wade?" Richardson sputtered. "El Halcon! The danged owlhoot who's always horning in on some good thing and skimming off the cream!"

"Yes, I'm sure," Ballard replied composedly. "He's El Halcon, all right; the hellion nobody can kill! Now you see how much chance you'd have with him in a corpse and cartridge session. And, though as to this I'm not wholly convinced and may put it to the test some time, plenty of folks will tell you he's got the fastest gunhand in the whole Southwest. But what he has got is something more important — a fast, keen mind that doesn't often make mistakes. It's not so much that he outshoots the opposition, he out-thinks them."

One of the men at the table spoke up nervously. "Ballard, I don't like it," he said. "I tell you he's not a man, he's a devil, and the bullet ain't run that can kill him. I'd rather have the rangers after me than that ice-eyed hellion."

Ballard smiled thinly as he cheerfully dropped another bombshell.

"Don't let that angle bother you," he said. "El Halcon is a Texas Ranger!"

Consternation really took over. Richardson gasped and swore. "Wade, you don't mean that?" he gulped. "Why, everybody knows he's an owlhoot —"

"You mean a lot of people think he is," Ballard corrected. "I happen to know he's Jim McNelty's lieutenant and ace-man who works under cover whenever he can. Oh, yes, he's a ranger. See what we're up against?"

"I'm beginning to think this whole danged oil business is a mistake," said another. "We were doing all right as it was, and the saloon pays off pretty well, too."

"Chicken feed!" scoffed Ballard. "If we work things right we'll all be sitting pretty for life and nothing to worry about."

"Do you think he's caught on to what we're after?" asked Richardson.

"I rather doubt it, although it's not beyond the realm of possibility," Ballard replied. "He's plenty smart, all right."

"And I'm beginning to darn near believe Cort may have the right of it, and he is a devil," growled Richardson, his face working.

"Well, man or devil, he's got to be eliminated," Ballard stared with decision. "Oh, stop having a fit and sit down here and listen; I've got an idea. The first thing to remember is that he rides alone a lot."

Richardson seated himself beside Ballard and the voices lowered to an almost inaudible mutter.

FOURTEEN

The following afternoon Slade got the rig on Shadow; he wanted another look at the hills to the east. Figuring that he might be late getting back to the ranchhouse he stowed some food alongside the little flat bucket and the small skillet that always reposed in his saddle pouch. He had just finished these preparations when Mary Mawson appeared leading a chunky bay.

"I want to go with you," she announced.

"Okay," he agreed, "but get your slicker," he told her, glancing at the lowering sky; "looks like we may have rain before the day's over."

"I've got it strapped back of my saddle," she replied.

They set off at a fast pace that soon left the ranchhouse behind. They rode east by south until the canyon-slashed hills were close. Slade studied the hills intently. In terms of geological age they were undoubtedly very old, but he was convinced that the gradual lowering to the north was not due to weathering away. The slope of the rim-rock was as it had been in the far-off day of the inland sea, always from south to north.

He glanced westward and his gaze fixed on a clump of grove perhaps a thousand yards distant.

"What are you looking at, Walt?" Mary asked.

"Something moving around the edge of those trees over there."

Mary strained her eyes. "I don't see anything," she said.

"You will in a minute," Slade predicted. "See?"

From the shadow of the grove bulged seven horsemen riding at a swift pace.

"Must be some of the boys," Mary guessed.

"They're all up at the north pastures today," Slade answered, his brows drawing together as he watched the hard riding troop lessen the distance. He didn't like the looks of that steady, purposeful approach and experienced an uneasy feeling that he and his companion were on an unpleasant spot. Had he been alone, and forking Shadow, he would have given the matter little consideration, confident as he was in the black's great speed and endurance; but Mary's bay, while a good horse, was certainly not built for speed.

"Mary," he said abruptly, "turn your horse and ride straight for the hills, and stay in front of me. Don't ask questions, ride!"

She shot him a puzzled look, but obeyed without protest. Slade crowded close behind her so as to provide as much of a shield as possible with his own body. He glanced back over his shoulder.

"Thought so!" he muttered.

From the ranks of the speeding horsemen puffed whitish smoke. A bullet sang overhead.

"Good heavens!" cried the girl. "Are they shooting at us?"

"They aren't doing anything else," Slade answered. "Head for that canyon mouth straight ahead. Fast as you can. Ride!"

Mary put spurs to the bay and he darted forward, Shadow crowding his heels. More slugs whined past, but the distance was still too great for anything like accurate shooting.

"Maybe they wouldn't shoot a woman but at a distance they can't tell that you are one," Slade shouted. "Ride!"

The canyon mouth was close. It was narrow and bristling with dead-looking growth that tossed and swayed in the draught sucking down the gorge. Slade didn't like that steady draught; it hinted that the canyon was a box, heated air rising from its narrow confines and being replaced by cool air that rushed down to escape through the mouth. But it was the only refuge that offered.

Into the growth they crashed, heedless of twigs and thorns and raking branches.

"Get your head down!" he told Mary. "Snug behind your horse's neck and keep going!"

The canyon floor sloped upward gently and if it was a box, doubtless at its head the growth would be thin, which wouldn't help matters.

They covered something over half a mile of hard going when the growth did begin to thin. A moment later Slade swore bitterly; the canyon was a box, walled by perpendicular cliffs. He glanced anxiously to left and right.

The slope on the left, he decided, could be climbed by a horse, slowly, but the growth on it was sparse and up there they would be perfect targets from the canyon floor. Very quickly the pursuit would realize the fugitives were trapped and would steal forward through the growth to surround them. He grimly loosened his heavy Winchester in the saddle boot. He'd try and make some kind of a stand in the brush.

First, however, he headed straight for the end wall, over a practically denuded stretch where only a few scattered bushes strove for rootage in the stony soil. There might be some crevice in which they could find dubious shelter.

But he quickly saw the cliff was unbroken. With the bay jostling beside him, he pulled Shadow to a halt, turned him and glanced about, and as his eyes rested on the tinder dry growth rustling in the draught he evolved a desperate expedient. The draught down the canyon appeared to be steady and he doubted if anything would cause it to alter its direction. They might both pay with their lives if he was mistaken, but he decided to take the chance. He knew very well his own life was forfeit if the pursuers caught up with them and they would hardly leave the girl alive, even did they realize she was a girl, as a witness to the killing. He swung to the ground.

"Hold the horses," he told Mary. "I don't think they'll run, but things are going to be lively hereabouts in a minute."

Running back to the edge of the growth, he plucked out his bottle of matches, struck one and held the tiny flicker to the dry grass and weeds that grew beside the bushes. A flame leaped up and crackled fiercely in the wind. Within seconds it was licking the dead lower branches.

Slade ran a little distance and kindled another fire, raced back the other way and added still a third to the growing conflagration. His keen ears detected the pound and crash of approaching horses.

"You'll be headed the other way pronto," he muttered as he straightened up and pocketed his matches. Above the crackle of the flames he heard startled yells and a prodigious crashing. By the time he reached his horse and mounted, a wall of fire stretched clear across the narrow gorge.

"As soon as the smoke gets thick we'll tackle that slope on the left," he told Mary. "Stay close to the cliff, it's going to be hotter'n the devil up here in a little bit." He rode forward a few paces the better to study the slope.

There was a clatter of hoofs, a scream from Mary. Through the wall of fire burst a horseman, face burned and blackened, eyes glaring. His clothes smoked and smoldered. The big dun he rode, mad with pain and terror, plunged frantically forward in a blind endeavor to escape the searing flame. Shoulder to shoulder he struck Shadow.

Down went both horses, kicking and squealing. Their riders were hurled free and struck the ground side by side. The dun's rider whipped out a gun. Slade lunged for it, caught the other's wrist as the gun blazed; the bullet fanned his face, burning powder stung his cheek. The outlaw streaked for his second gun but Slade pinned his hand against his holster and held on.

Mary leaped from her saddle, ran to where Shadow, who had scrambled to his feet, stood snorting and blowing, and jerked Slade's Winchester from the boot but could not use it because the two bodies were so closely intertwined. Clubbing the rifle by the barrel she glided forward and waited her chance.

Over and over rolled the fighters, butting, kicking, kneeing. Slade did not dare loose the owlhoot's wrists and he was badly shaken by the fall. All he could do for the moment was prevent the other from lining sights with him.

The fellow was a big man, heavier by many pounds than the tall ranger, and he seemed to be made of steel and rawhide. Slowly, slowly he brought his wrist down, twisting the gun sideways till the muzzle was almost against Slade's head. He pulled trigger a second time and Slade felt the burn of that one along his temple. Lights blazed before his eyes, followed by a swirling blackness. With every atom of his strength, he twisted the other's wrist sideways and down. He gave a mighty jerk and at that instant the outlaw's finger tightened again on the trigger.

The big Colt boomed, there was a gasping, choking cry; blood spurted over Slade's arm. The other's body jerked and twitched, the gun dropped from his hand.

For a moment the convulsive movements persisted, then the man went limp; he had shot himself through the throat.

His brain whirling, flashes of red and black streaming before his eyes, Slade struggled to his feet, dimly aware that Mary was clinging to him, supporting him. His mind cleared quickly as he gulped great draughts of the hot, smoky air.

"Are you all right, Walt? Are you all right?" she was crying.

"Sure," he mumbled. "I'm fine."

"There's blood on your face!"

"Just a scratch," he reassured her. "I'll be okay in another minute."

His head was indeed clearing swiftly. He glanced toward the wall of fire now some distance down the canyon. The heat was blistering but it would quickly ease off. He glanced again at the fire. It was travelling too darn fast for comfort. Soon the light growth would be burned out and the outlaws would be able to return up the canyon.

"Come on," he told the girl, "we've got to tackle that slope on the left and get up it before the smoke clears and those hellions come back looking for us."

Mary picked up the fallen rifle and handed it to him. "I never got a chance to use it," she said. She shuddered a little as she glanced at the distorted face of the dead outlaw, but her blue eyes flashed.

"One less murderer in the world, anyhow," she said.

"Mary," Slade chuckled, "you're a girl to ride the river with!"

It was hard going up the slope. They coughed and choked in the thick smoke that rolled upward in clouds. The horses blew and snorted, their irons slipping on the stones, but forged ahead steadily until Slade knew they could be no great distance from the crest. It was just about sunset and before the smoke cloud cleared darkness would cover their retreat.

And then the weather gods, which are a perverse and unpredictable bunch, decided to take a hand. Already there had been grumbles of thunder overhead. A breath of wind stirred the billows of smoke. Another came, stronger than the first. Overhead sounded a deep rumble. Then came a rustling that swelled and swelled to a mighty roar as the stirring giant of the storm sprang into raging life. Twigs and leaves pelted Slade and the girl. Branches snapped under the force of the blast. The wind tore at their clothes, threatening to strip them from their backs. Clouds of dust billowed down from the bare slope above to join the rolling smoke. The black heavens were split asunder by a jagged flame that fell to the earth in a torrent of fire. The crash of the thunder followed and with its bellow came a veritable cataract of water driven in level lances by the wind. Almost instantly the eerie twilight faded into darkness through which the lightning blazed, the thunder rolled and the torrent of rain blotted out all things.

Blinded, deafened by the lashing rain and the infernal uproar, Slade gripped the bay's bridle iron, fearful lest they be separated in the black turmoil.

"Hang on!" he shouted to Mary and urged Shadow forward.

"I think we'd be better off down below," she screamed through the turmoil.

"Can't risk it," Slade shouted. "Those hellions will come sneaking back up the canyon now the rain's put the fire out; the storm won't stop them. We've got to reach the rim-rock and get in the clear before they figure out where we went. They won't give up as long as they think they have a chance to run us down. And they'd be sure to come looking for the one they're short, or what's left of him."

"I wonder how that one got through the fire?" she asked.

"Chances are his horse ran away with him," Slade replied. "Fire drives horses loco some times; they'll run right into it. Save your breath, you're going to need it."

Now they were climbing the bare upper slope and exposed to the full fury of the storm. Beaten and buffeted, the terrified horses struggled up the last sag, and after what seemed an eternity reached the rim-rock and staggered across its level surface.

"We can't stand much of this, got to find shelter!" Slade yelled to his companion. "Hang on! We must keep going!"

Her voice came back thin as the piping of an insect in the uproar, "Don't worry! I'm right with you!"

Another blaze of lightning showed a huge boulder directly ahead. Slade made for it and in its lee they managed to unstrap and struggle into their slickers. They were drenched to the skin but the stout garments protected them somewhat from the awful beat of wind and rain. Then they forged ahead once more, blindly seeking for a cliff or overhang that would provide something of shelter.

Suddenly Shadow halted, snorting and blowing. Slade's grip on the bit iron curbed the bay. The lightning blazed and revealed, at their very feet, the sheer drop of a canyon wall. Down the far canyon wall roared a mighty torrent of water. The canyon itself was half filled with a tossing, foam-flecked flood, its heaving surface dotted by logs and uprooted trees. The cliffs stood out like bursts of frozen flame. Thrashing trees writhed and contorted in black agony.

Down came the darkness. Slade did not dare move till he got his bearings. The horses moaned and shivered.

Another lightning bolt flashed flame across the wild heavens. Slade backed Shadow away from the sheer drop to the raging torrent below and started him at an angle that widened away from the canyon. Utterly confused they fought their way through the flame streaked darkness. They heard the crash of falling trees, were hammered by spouts of water gushing over the uprearing rocks. They were utterly lost and seemed to be wandering through some unlimited eternity of sound and fury and numbing pain.

Then unexpectedly the beat of wind and rain lessened greatly. Shadow veered a little, then shambled on. A lightning flash revealed a wall of cliffs, along the base of which they were riding. Directly ahead was a deep overhang. A few more minutes and they were under the shelf of rock. The lightning flashed again and Slade saw a black opening in the cliff face.

"A cave!" he shouted to Mary. "This is a break! Wait a minute."

He dismounted and groped his way into the opening. He wrung the water from his hand and felt of the rock wall. It was perfectly dry. From an inner pocket he fumbled his bottle of matches which he was confident had escaped the general wetting. Shaking one forth, he scratched it on the wall. The flame revealed a flat rock floor sloping slightly outward. It also revealed heaps of leaves and twigs driven in from time to time by the wind. He scraped a pile together. They were tinder dry and when he applied the flame of a second match they burned up brightly. He scooped up more twigs and fed the blaze.

"Ride in and bring Shadow with you," he shouted to Mary. "We're in clover."

Gratefully the exhausted horses shambled into the cave. The girl dismounted stiffly. Her teeth were chattering like castanets and she was numb with cold, but she managed him a rather wan smile.

"Get your slicker off and hunker close to the fire," Slade told her. "Now you keep it going with this stuff I've raked together. I saw brush growing along the base of the cliff. I'll go out there and bust loose some heavy stuff to make a real blaze."

He groped along the base of the cliff till he encountered the growth. Then he quickly broke off an armload of dead lower branches. They were damp but the heat of the burning leaves and twigs quickly dried them and they caught fire. Soon a very respectable blaze was going. Slade brought load after load of fuel from the growth until the flames were soaring to the rock roof and the shallow cave was delightfully warm.

"I'll pack in a few more loads of the heaviest stuff I can find to keep her going and then we'll eat," Slade told the girl. "How you feel?"

"Oh, I feel wonderful now," she replied. "I'm perfectly warm and I'm drying out. And anyhow we're safe from those danged drygulchers. I hope they all got burned up or drowned or something."

Slade chuckled and went for more wood. A few more loads and he decided they had enough to keep the fire going for several hours. Next he got the drenched rigs off the horses and stacked them against the wall. He hauled the provisions from the saddle pouch and laid them out. Mary got busy with the skillet while he filled the bucket from a stream of water pouring down the outer rock. Soon bacon was crisping, eggs frying and coffee bubbling.

With the resilience of youth and perfect physical condition, both had thrown off their fatigue and they laughed merrily over the just past harrowing experiences as they sat on the bed of leaves they had raked together and ate their simple meal. Full fed and content, Mary stretched out beside the fire and smiled up at him.

"This is perfectly cozy," she said.

FIFTEEN

The gray light of dawn was seeping into the cave when Slade awoke. Mary was still sleeping sweetly. He arose noiselessly so as not to disturb her and went outside for a look at the sky. The storm was over, the air perfectly still and the world green and fresh with morning. Remembering that there was still some coffee left he filled the bucket with water from a depression in the rock and started getting a fire going.

Mary awoke and sat up, knuckling her eyes. She ran her fingers through her tousled curls and gave a moan of despair.

"The sight I must look!" she wailed.

"What I was wondering," Slade said, "was how the devil a girl can look so darn pretty this early in the morning."

"Nice of you to say it, but I don't believe you," she replied. "I can't get my eyes open!"

"There's a puddle right outside, go douse 'em in that," Slade told her.

"I will," she said, and scrambled from the cave. She was back in a few minutes rosy and panting.

"Here, have some coffee," Slade said, "that will wake you up."

They drank the coffee and while Mary washed the utensils in the pool of water outside the cave, Slade got the rigs on the horses. He soon got his bearings and found a way down the slopes. Less than two hours later they were out on the prairie. They had covered a couple more miles when they sighted a group of horsemen riding swiftly from the north.

"This is getting too frequent to be funny

any more," Slade growled as he loosened the Winchester in its scabbard.

"Do you think it could be those men again?" Mary asked apprehensively.

"I don't know," Slade replied. "I didn't figure they'd hang around out here after daylight, but you never can tell about such a bunch. Get behind me and stay there."

A moment later, however, he uttered an exclamation of relief. "It's your dad and the boys, riding down here to shoot me for keeping you out all night, I expect," he said.

They rode on steadily to meet the advancing troop. Old Tom jerked his blowing horse to a sliding halt.

"What the devil happened?" he demanded. "I've been worried half to death."

"Oh, the rain caught us and we decided to spend the night in a cave," Mary explained blithely.

Her father snorted. "Can't you be serious for a minute? Walt, what did happen?"

But it was Mary who told him, vividly. Mawson and the punchers shook their heads and muttered oaths as the tale progressed. When it was finished, Mawson turned to Slade.

"Walt," he said, "it seems this whole family keeps getting deeper and deeper in debt to you all the time."

When they reached the ranchhouse and he had a chance to talk with Slade alone, old Tom took a very serious view of the matter.

"They're out to get you, son," he said. "It's a bad bunch that will stop at nothing. I'm worried."

"Well, they haven't had much luck so far," Slade answered, "and they are getting sort of whittled down. If I can keep on accounting for one or two each time they tangle with me, after a while there won't be any left."

"Yes, if your luck doesn't run out on you," Mawson grunted. "I'm beginning to be scairt that maybe I made a mistake when I persuaded you to stay on here."

Slade was silent for a few minutes. He was thinking things over and he abruptly arrived at a decision. He fumbled with a cunningly hidden secret pocket in his broad leather belt and laid something on the table between them. It was a gleaming silver star set on a silver circle, the feared and honored badge of the Texas Rangers!

Old Tom stared at the symbol of law and order. "Well, I'll be darned!" he rumbled. "So that's what you are! I might have known it — you do things like a ranger."

Suddenly his eyes widened. "Say, something's beginning to click!" he exclaimed. "Walt Slade! I thought that name sounded sort of familiar when I first heard it, but there are lots of Slades in Texas and I didn't think anything of it at the time. Aren't you the ranger they call El Halcon?"

"I have been called that," Slade admitted.

Old Tom gazed almost in awe at the man whose exploits were legend throughout the Southwest.

"El Halcon!" he repeated. "The ranger nobody can kill! No wonder those hellions ain't been having any luck with you. Well, if this don't take the hide off the barn door. And McNelty sent you over here, eh? I wrote to him and I've been wondering why I didn't hear anything. I couldn't think old Jim would let me down. I knew him back in the old days before he was a ranger."

"Captain Jim never lets anybody down," Slade replied. "He got your letter, and letters from the oilmen, too, incidentally, and he thought it might be a good notion for me to drop over here and have a look-see."

"And do you know who's reponsible for the hell-raising?" Mawson asked eagerly.

"Yes, I think I know," Slade admitted, "but knowing isn't proving, and that's just how the situation stands at present. I think Wade Ballard is the brains behind the outfit, with

Blaine Richardson as his field man, and the devil knows how many other hellions working with him, although I don't believe there are overly many. They operate like a comparatively small, close-knit bunch."

"Wade Ballard!" Mawson repeated incredulously. "He always struck me as a purty nice sort of feller. What the devil has he got against me?"

"Nothing," Slade replied, "but you've got something he wants — the Walking M spread."

"The Walking M!" Mawson exclaimed. "Tarnation, he ain't no cattleman."

"No," Slade agreed, "but in my opinion he is an oilman and a darned smart engineer who probably got kicked out of legitimate practice because of something off-color he pulled. That, of course, is just surmise on my part, but I'd be willing to bet money on it."

"But if he ain't a cattleman, why does he want the Walking M bad enough to be willing to commit murder to get it?"

"That," Slade replied, "I'll discuss with you later. I want Bob Kent to be present when I do. Do you mind if I bring him up here?"

"I can even put up with an oilman if you ask me to," growled old Tom.

"I've a notion you'll find him a pretty good sort, just as you found Arch Caldwell a pretty good sort," Slade predicted.

Mawson looked dubious but did not argue the point. "And do you think you can figure a way to drop a loop on the side-winders?" he asked.

"I think perhaps I can, with Kent's help and yours."

"Well, you'll get mine, anything I can do," Mawson declared. "Where does Kent come in on the deal?"

"He provides the know-how," Slade answered, adding with a smile, "and you provide the money, or part of it."

"Well, I ain't got over much right now, but every cent I can lay my hands on you're welcome to," Mawson instantly agreed.

"It'll be very much in the nature of a gamble," Slade said. "But unless I'm mistaken, and I don't think I am, and you draw the right card to fill your inside straight, you'll never have to worry about money again."

"I always sort of liked to gamble," chuckled Mawson. "And after all, what can an old jigger like me do for fun except guzzle whiskey and gamble? Oh, to be sixty again!"

The following morning, Slade rode to Weirton and hunted up Bob Kent.

"Want you to take a little ride with me, Bob," he announced.

"Sure," responded Kent. "Where to?"

"Up to visit Tom Mawson."

Kent looked considerably startled. "What you got against me that you want me to get shot?" he demanded.

"I don't think you'll get shot, at least not at the Walking M," Slade smiled. "In fact, I'll guarantee you won't."

"Okay," Kent agreed dubiously. "I only hope you just haven't had too much of the Black Gold's tarantula juice and are suffering from some sort of delusions."

They didn't get shot on the way to the Walking M, nor after they got there. Old Tom received Kent cordially enough and they sat down to dinner together. Later Mary whispered to Slade, "You're a miracle worker if there ever was one. An oilman sitting at Dad's table!"

Sixteen

After they repaired to the living room and cigarettes were lighted, Kent and Mawson glanced expectantly at Slade. He smoked in silence for several moments before speaking, his eyes deep in thought. First he laid his ranger star on the table. Kent's eyes goggled.

"Well, I'll be hanged!" he exclaimed.

"Hope so," Slade returned cheerfully, "but we'll talk about other things before we take that up. I feel a little explanation of conditions here as I see them is first in order. Bob, your deductions relative to this section were accurate, so far as you went! This whole valley was at one time an inland sea, but as I told you, the desert to the south never was. To begin with, I want you to recall in your mind the contours of the hills to the east and west, the hills that once formed the high shoreline of the inland sea. You will realize that the slope of this whole section was once from south to north."

Kent's brows drew together and he thought for a moment. "Darned if I don't believe you're right about the hills, now that you call it to my attention," he said, "but the slope of the valley is definitely from north to south."

"Just so," Slade agreed, "the slope of the hills is still south to north as it always was. But in the course of upheavals after the drying up of the sea water, or possibly even before, the surface trend of the basin reversed, while that of the hills remained the same."

"Sounds logical," Kent admitted. Mawson

nodded his understanding.

Slade paused again, then spoke slowly, choosing his words with care. "Remember now, what's coming is my own personal deduction based on a survey of the terrain and the peculiar phenomena manifesting themselves subsequent to Kent's initial oil strike; I wouldn't venture to advance it as a positive statement of fact, although I'm confident in my own mind that I'm right. In my opinion the reversal of slope obtained to no great depth, geologically speaking. The trend of the lower levels remains the same as when the sea was in existence. And the lower trend governed the formation of the oil pool that underlies the valley. Begin to see what I'm getting at, Bob?"

"I believe I do," Kent replied, his eyes glowing with excitement, "but keep on talking."

"Okay," Slade said. "In my opinion what you drilled into, Bob, was a mere backwash that flowed over a subterranean ridge in the course of the creation of the deposit to form the pool your wells tapped. That's why your pressure eased off so quickly. The pool is comparatively small and because it was a backwash and was not originally closely confined, it never developed any great pressure."

"I'm beginning to get it!" Kent exclaimed, "but go ahead."

"So in my opinion, the main and deepest reservoir is not under the mesa, but up here to the north. In other words, if my deduction is correct, Mr. Mawson has got a fortune under his land."

"The devil you say!" exploded old Tom.

"Mr. Mawson, I believe he's right," Kent exclaimed excitedly. "Tell us how you figured it out, Walt."

"That two-and-a-half-mile strip of spoiled grass and the scum of oil on the creek puzzled me," Slade explained. "To me, it didn't make sense to think that it was caused by seepage from the oil field on the mesa. But still I couldn't understand it till one day I realized that the rimrock slope was not from north to south but from south to north. That started me thinking hard on the matter and I arrived at certain conclusions. In my opinion there is a minor fault either following the course of the stream or slightly to the north of it. When Kent brought in his wells, the subterranean jolting and jarring in consequence doubtless widened that fault and extended it nearer the surface. Oil from the big reservoir up here, which is almost certain to be under great pressure, rushed into the fault and seeps through crevices into the water and up to the grass roots."

He paused to light a cigarette and then continued. "But I hesitated to mention my theory to anybody because there was, and is, a flaw in my reasoning. There is a bare possibility, remember I say a bare possibility, that the oil follows a fault from the pool under the mesa. Personally I don't believe it does, but even such a remote contingency caused me to be a bit reluctant to altogether trust my own judgment. Then all of a sudden I had my theory corroborated by somebody else."

"Who?" asked Kent.

"I'm coming to that," Slade smiled. "I had already arrived at the conclusion that somebody was out to ruin Mr. Mawson financially, to put him on very much of a spot for ready cash. His cows were poisoned and he had more stock widelooped than anybody else. Then when the attempt was made to destroy his big shipping herd in Hanging Rock Canyon, the thing was perfectly obvious. But who, and why? Then he told me that Wade Ballard had tried to buy land here to the north, giving him a cock-and-bull story about the railroad possibly planning to build shops and a big assembling yard down here. Right away I knew that Ballard had formed the same conclusion about the oil that I had."

"Wade Ballard!" Kent ejaculated. "Why he's just a saloon man."

"There is where you're very much wrong," Slade replied soberly. "Wade Ballard is a brilliant engineer or scientist who somehow took to riding a crooked trail. Wade Ballard knows there's a fortune under the Walking M and he and his sidekick Blaine Richardson are out to get it."

Kent shook his head in amazement. "I'm not surprised about Richardson, but Ballard always struck me as a pretty nice feller," he said.

"He's got plenty of personal charm to go along with his intelligence," Slade conceded. "He has the ability to get along with most everybody. Even Mr. Mawson got to thinking pretty well of him."

A thought struck Kent. "But why is Richardson drilling a well out on the desert?" he asked.

"As a blind," Slade replied. "To attract attention away from up here. Ballard knows that there is always a chance of somebody stumbling onto what he has learned. You didn't get very far with your scientific education, Bob, but Ballard doubtless fears you got far enough to possibly figure the thing out, especially if the production of your wells starts falling off, as I figure it will before long, and you get to wondering where the devil the oil went that you know should be here. But with you and the other oilmen running circles around yourselves out on the desert you wouldn't be giving any thought to the land north of the creek. Richardson has been doing the spade work against just such a contingency."

"I bet it was Richardson fired those wells!" Kent exclaimed.

"Naturally," Slade said. "Part of the plan to keep the cattlemen and oilmen on the prod against each other and to lessen the possibility of an oilman buying land north of the creek. That's where they slipped, though. I was convinced that somebody connected with the oil field fired the wells. No cowhand would have the know-how."

"Are you going to grab the scoundrels and throw 'em in the calaboose?" Kent asked.

Slade smiled a little. "On what charge?"

"Why — why I guess murder would do as well as any other," Kent replied. "They killed one of Mr. Mawson's cowboys, didn't they? And two men died when that first well was fired. And there have been several other killings in the section that I'll bet they're responsible for."

"I'll agree with you on all counts," Slade said, "but how about proof? A theory as to why Wade Ballard wants Mr. Mawson's land? He tried to buy it open and above board, didn't he? And gave his reason for wanting to do so. 'No bill' says the grand jury. An oil-soaked cap Clate Mawson shot off the head of one of the bunch who tried to kill him on the rimrock trail, a cow thief's pocket with oily grit caked in the lining, and I haven't even got a cow thief to go with it. Try and sell that kind of a bill of goods to a jury! I'm convinced in my own mind that Nate Persinger, Richardson's driller, tried to kill me that night in the Black Gold, but fifty people who were there will swear that Persinger shot at Bill Ayers, not at me. I thought I saw a chance to tangle Richardson's twine for him when those two hellions tried to drygulch me on the Chihuahua Trail, but he was too damn smart. No way to connect the two drygulchers with him. Not even by association. Nobody ever saw them in Richardson's company, nor in Ballard's either, for that matter. Oh, it's a shrewd bunch, all right, shrewd and deadly, but an organization like that always has a weak spot which is very often its undoing, as I hope it may be in this case. It takes money to hold such a bunch together and

195

the head of the gang has to plan and pull jobs to get it if he wants to keep his men in hand. I'll take up that angle a little later, but right now I come to what I have in mind."

He paused, eyed his listeners for a moment, and resumed, "Mr. Mawson, I want you and Bob to drill a well on your land."

Old Tom looked considerably startled. Bob Kent gave a whistle.

"As I told Mr. Mawson, it's something in the nature of a gamble," Slade continued. "If you win, Mr. Mawson, you'll have plenty of money to take care of your debts and enable you to keep on lending a helping hand to others, as I've learned you've been doing all your life. If I'm right in my conclusions, when Bob's wells down on the mesa start petering out, he'll be in on the ground floor of a new and bigger strike. If I'm all wrong and you lose, well you can figure that out for yourself, consider it, and act accordingly."

Old Tom tugged his mustache and chuckled. "As I told you last night, son, I always did like a gamble," he said. "I reckon it'll just about empty my poke but I'm with you till the last brand's run. What do you say, Kent?"

"Sure I'll go along," the oilman declared

heartily. "I risked my last cent down on the mesa and I'm ready to risk it again. I reckon I'll be doing that all my life," he added with a grin, "and quite probably end up like my dad did — busted; but I'll have had a lot of fun."

"And if we hit the jackpot we'll split three ways," said Mawson. "I figure Walt will have earned his share."

Walt Slade smiled and shook his head. "I'm much obliged," he said, "but I've got a few *pesos* stashed away and a man in my line of work doesn't need much money. All I ask is a chance to drop a loop on the sidewinders who have been raising the devil in this section. That's my chore and I'll get plenty of satisfaction out of completing it. Now I'll tell you how to work things.

"Mr. Mawson, you spread the news around, especially in Weirton, that Kent has convinced you there is oil under your land and that you've decided to gamble a certain amount on the possibility. Kent can estimate the cost pretty closely and let you know how much to say. Make it clear that you are prepared to go just so far and no farther, that if he can't get results with what you put up the deal is off and the project will be abandoned; you should be able to make it sound convincing. It's pretty well-known that you can use some extra money and it won't seem illogical that you're willing to risk a certain investment on the hope of getting it. I believe that when Ballard and Richardson hear about it, they'll get panicky and possibly tip their hand, even if I don't figure a way to make them do it before."

"I'm with you," old Tom repeated. "What's the other angle you mentioned?"

"My expectation that they'll try and pull something shortly to replenish their exchequer," Slade replied. "Losing that herd of yours they thought they had must have made the rank and file members a bit disgruntled. Ballard will have to plan something to keep them quiet, even though the chances are that right now he'd rather not. If I can only anticipate what they have in mind I may be able to lay a trap for them. You're familiar with conditions in the section, Mr. Mawson, can you think of anything that might look like easy pickings to an outlaw bunch?"

Old Tom pulled his mustache and thought. "By gosh, I believe I've got it!" he exclaimed. "Tol Releford of the Bradded R is getting a shipping herd together. He has a contract with the packers and they want cows in place of the two hundred that he lost in Hanging Rock Canyon and they

198

didn't get. Need 'em to fill their orders, and more, too. Tol figures to get about five hundred together. That might be just the thing the hellions will make a try for. Everybody knows Tol is careless as the devil about money matters and everything else. He'll hold that herd in a corral he has built on his east pasture and won't even go to the trouble to post a night guard. What do you think?"

"I think it's something else worth gambling on," Slade said slowly. "Do you think Releford will work with us?"

"Sure he will, if he thinks there's a chance to get into a fight," Mawson replied. "That hunk of tallow would rather fight than eat. You can count on Tol. I'll ride up there first thing in the morning and have a talk with him. Shall I tell him you're a ranger?"

"Yes, I think you'd better, but tell him to keep it under his hat," Slade replied. "I'm still figuring that maybe those hellions don't know for sure that I am. I hope they don't, anyhow."

"Okay, I'll put a flea in Tol's ear," Mawson promised. "You can depend on him to keep his mouth shut."

"Fine!" Slade applauded. "Well, I guess that about takes care of everything."

"We'll have a couple of drinks on it," said

Mawson, producing a bottle, "and then I reckon a little shut-eye is in order. Bob, you can sleep in the room across from mine at the far end of the hall. Poor Jess Rader used to squat there but he's sleeping under the pines up on the hill, now. I sure hope I get a chance to even up for Jess."

After the drinks were downed, Kent and old Tom headed for bed. Slade sat smoking and thinking for some time. Presently he blew out the light and also went upstairs.

SEVENTEEN

Early the following morning, Mawson rode up to the Bradded R. He was back before noon.

"Tol will go along with us," he announced. "I knew he would. Let's have something to eat and then Bob and me'll ride to town and spread the news around."

There was plenty of excitement and plenty of arguing when it was learned that Tom Mawson planned to drill a well on his property. The general consensus of opinion among the oilmen was that Mawson was loco and Bob Kent, who ought to know better, was more so. Again and again it was pointed out that the slope of the valley was from north to south, proof positive that the only deposit was under the mesa. Unless, as some were inclined to agree, Blaine Richardson had the right idea and the larger pool was beneath the desert, the elevation of which, it was also pointed out, was greatly less than that of the mesa.

Richardson himself bellowed with laughter when he heard the news and declared that Kent and Mawson were as shy of brains as a terrapin of feathers.

That was Richardson's public face. It was quite different in the course of another meeting in the back room of the Black Gold saloon.

"Either Kent or that dang Slade figured the thing out and sold Mawson the notion," he declared. "And where does it leave us — holding the bag!"

Growls ran around the table. Only Wade Ballard, smiling as usual and toying with a cigarette, did not appear particularly perturbed. "Stop worrying about it," he said. "Let them go ahead and drill. Everything will be taken care of at the right time. Mawson will never strike oil."

"And meanwhile we're just about busted and the boys need money," Richardson growled.

"They'll get it," Ballard replied. "I'm taking care of that, too, and without delay."

"What you got in mind?" Richardson asked.

"Tol Releford's shipping herd is what I'm thinking about," Ballard answered. "Five hundred head of first-class beefs almost ready to take the trail, and the old fool doesn't even post a night guard at the corral."

Richardson stared at him, his face working. "Tol Releford's shipping herd!" he repeated incredulously. "And do you figure for a minute that Slade hasn't thought of that?"

"Doubtless he has," Ballard returned composedly.

"Uh-huh, and anybody trying to lift that herd will end up blown from under his hat!" Richardson snorted. "What's the matter with you, anyhow?"

"My dear Richardson," Ballard replied smoothly, "don't think that because you were behind the door when they were handing out brains that everybody was. If everything goes off per schedule, and I see no reason why it won't, what I have in mind will be easy as rolling off a slick log. Of course, Slade will have figured out that we are likely to make a try for that herd — it's the only thing worthwhile lying around loose at the moment. Of course he'll be waiting there with a bunch. Let him wait. It won't get him anything except perhaps a bad cold from staying out at night."

"Oh, tarnation, stop putting the spurs to me and let's hear what you've got to say!" demanded Richardson.

But as Ballard's low voice unfolded his plan, scowls were replaced by grins of anticipation. Even Richardson's glowering features relaxed.

"Feller, you're smart!" he admitted grudgingly. "I got to hand it to you, you're smart, darn smart!"

After the others had departed, Richardson remarked, "If something goes haywire with that scheme of yours it's danged likely to be curtains for the boys."

Ballard shrugged his shoulders. "What of it!" he replied callously, "plenty more of that sort to be had if we should happen to need them. The way things are going," he added, "soon only you and I and Nate Persinger will know what we have in mind."

"And that might be one too many," Richardson observed significantly.

"Exactly," Ballard agreed. "I'll consider that at the proper time."

The way he said it seemed to have a disquieting effect on Richardson. His eyes slid away from Ballard's and he moved uneasily in his chair.

Two days later the last cow that made up the Bradded R shipping herd was safe in the corral. The following morning the herd would take the trail.

"And do you really think those hellions will make a try for it tonight?" Mawson asked Slade.

"Yes, I'm pretty sure of it now," Slade replied. "All day somebody way up in the hills over there has been keeping tabs on us. I spotted him twice where the brush was a bit thin. He did a good chore of keeping under cover, but not quite good enough. Nobody on any legitimate business would be riding around up there."

Night came with a slice of moon casting a wan light over the rangeland. Slade and the Bradded R outfit, all except Stiffy Cole, the cook, lay concealed in a grove near the corral. With them were Mawson and Bob Kent, who had insisted on coming along. The night was very still, with only the contented grunting and grumbling of the cattle to break the silence.

The hours passed slowly and tediously until it was nearing midnight. Tol Releford grew pessimistic.

"I'm scairt your hunch ain't a straight

one, son," he said to Slade. "If they figured on anything they'd oughta been here before now. A little more and they wouldn't have time to get into the hills before daylight."

"I still think it will work out," Slade replied.

A little later Mawson cocked his head in an attitude of listening. "Don't I hear horses coming this way?" he whispered.

"You hear one horse, coming from the north and coming darned fast," Slade corrected. "Now what the devil does this mean?"

Tensely alert, the posse waited, while the beat of fast hoofs grew louder and louder until suddenly from behind a thicket bulged a single horseman, a hatless long and lanky individual who rode with his elbows flopping grotesquely and his disordered hair gleaming white in the moonlight.

"It's Stiffy Cole!" Releford bellowed. "You loco pelican, what the devil's the matter with you?"

"They got it!" bawled Stiffy, jerking his horse to a halt. "They busted open the safe and got the money!"

Tol Releford let out a roar of rage and a mouthful of profanity.

"What money?" Slade demanded. "What's he talking about?"

"The money for the cows!" Releford sputtered. "The buyer rode down from Proctor
and paid for 'em, like he always does. It was
in the living room safe."

"Why in blazes didn't you tell me?" Slade
demanded.

"Why, I didn't think of it," Releford
replied. "I always handle the business that
way. Have for years. Everybody knows it."

"I never thought of it, either," broke in
Tom Mawson.

Slade turned to the cook. "Stiffy, tell us
what happened," he said.

"I was in the kitchen working around the
stove when five buzzards wearing masks
busted in and grabbed me before I could
do a dang thing. They tied me up and went
into the living room and hammered open
that old tin box Tol keeps his money in.
Then they hightailed. They didn't do a very
good job of tieing and I managed to wiggle
loose in four or five minutes after they left.

"But I know where they headed for," Stiffy
shouted above the storm of profanity. "They
were heading for Yardley over west of the
hills. They've got a hole-up over there and
aimed to make for it after they stopped in
the town a bit."

Tol Releford let out an exultant bellow.
"We'll get the hellions!" he said. "We've got

good horses and we'll ride 'em down before they get there. Come on!"

He was heading for his horse when Slade's voice stopped him. "Hold it!" the ranger ordered peremptorily. "There's something funny about this. Stiffy, how do you know they are heading for Yardley?"

"I heard 'em say so," Stiffy explained. "I could hear 'em talking in the living room and I heard them say it."

"They talked loud enough for you to hear all the way to the kitchen?"

"That's right," Stiffy answered.

"And they did a mighty poor job of hog-tieing you?" Slade persisted.

"Reckon they did," Stiffy admitted. "I didn't have no trouble getting loose in a hurry."

"Well, what the devil are we waiting for?" bawled Releford. "Come on, we'll catch 'em before they get to Yardley."

"They're not headed for Yardley," Slade stated positively.

"What?" exclaimed Releford.

"Can't you see it's a plant?" Slade explained impatiently. "Stiffy heard just what they intended him to hear. They tied him so he would be able to free himself in a few minutes, knowing he'd hightail here to tell us what happened. Then off we'd go to

207

Yardley, following a cold trail, while they, I'm willing to bet money, would amble comfortably down the Chihuahua to Weirton."

"Darned if I don't believe you're right," said Mawson.

"I'm sure I am," Slade replied. "Listen, they outsmarted us, all right. They evidently knew about the money for the cows being delivered today. Releford intimated it's pretty common knowledge that he does business that way. But maybe they outsmarted themselves. By heading straight south across the prairie I believe we've got a good chance to get ahead of them, hole up and wait for them to come along. By heading south across the range we'll bypass the big bends in the trail and lop off a lot of miles. Come on, let's go!"

"I'm going, too," declared Stiffy. "Slade, let me have your saddle gun. I ain't much good with a Colt, but with a long gun I can dot a lizard's eye at twenty paces."

Within minutes the posse was headed south by slightly west. Slade set the pace, holding Shadow back in deference to the mounts of the others. Given free rein, the great black would have quickly left the posse standing still.

Mile after mile flowed past under the

speeding hoofs. Slade steadily veered the troop westward after they passed where the trail over the hills joined the Chihuahua.

"I think after they pass the forks they'll take it easier, figuring they're safe," he told his companions. "We should be ahead of them now, or very soon."

But not until they were almost within sight of Weirton did he head directly west to the Chihuahua. They located a thicket close to the broad white ribbon of the trail and pulled up in its shadow.

"Now all we can do is wait," Slade said. "If my hunch is a straight one we should hear them coming before long."

The minutes dragged past tediously, with nerves strained to the breaking point. Slade was not altogether easy in his mind about what was to come. The outlaws were desperate men and doubtless skilled in the use of hardware, whereas he knew that most cowboys were anything but good shots. However, there was usually one or two in every outfit who could handle a gun and Mawson and Kent both knew one end of a Colt from the other.

The moon was almost down to the crest of the western hills, and still the trail lay silent and deserted. The occasional jingle of a bit iron sounded loud in the utter silence.

209

Then suddenly a faint clicking sound drifted from the north to louden quickly to the rhythmic beat of hoofs.

"It's them!" whispered Releford.

"We've got to be sure," Slade told him. "We can't go throwing lead at just anybody who happens along. But if the ball opens, make it good. I don't think they'll be taken without a fight. Steady now and let me do the talking."

On came the unseen horses. Another moment and they bulged into view. Slade rode forward. His voice rang out, "Halt! In the name of the State of Texas!"

The answer was a wild yell and the gleam of the moonlight on gun barrels. Slade's hands flashed down and up. His first shot boomed before the outlaws could open fire. Followed a horrific outburst of noise and flame and smoke. On either side of Slade the possemen fired as fast as they could pull trigger. Slade saw two of the outlaws fall, heard a cry of pain on his right, a choking grunt on his left. His big Colts bucked in his hands and a third saddle was emptied. Then a fourth man went down. The fifth, bending low in his saddle, flashed down the trail, bullets whining all about him. He was almost out of sixgun range when old Stiffy clamped the butt of Slade's Winchester to his shoulder. His eyes glanced along the sights. A riderless horse went careening across the prairie.

"Got him!" squalled Stiffy. "Look at him! He's still bouncing!"

Satisfied that the outlaws were all dead, Slade took stock of his own casualties. One cowboy had a broken arm, another a hole through the top of his shoulder. A third had suffered a leg wound that Slade didn't consider serious.

"Danged good thing we caught them off balance, though," he said to Mawson as he went to work on the wounded. "They were plenty salty."

"You're darn right," old Tom agreed. "Look, Tol's found his money sack. All there, Tol?"

"Every last dollar," whooped the Bradded R owner. "They didn't even take the wrappers off the bundles. This is what I call a good night's work."

"Lots you had to do with it!" snorted Stiffy. "You were hiding behind me all the time."

"A grass snake couldn't hide behind you, you worm-eaten splinter!" retorted Releford. "What's next?"

"Round up the horses and tie the bodies on them," Slade directed, giving a final pat to a bandage. "We'll pack them to town and let folks look them over."

When they arrived at Weirton the oil town's never ending night life was still going full blast. Excitement ran high as the grim cavalcade clattered along the main street to the deputy sheriff's office. Sid Hawkins was routed out of bed and the bodies placed on display to be viewed by a crowd that was constantly augmented by new arrivals. But nobody was able to identify any of the dead men. Several bartenders were of the opinion that they had served one or another at some time but were vague as to when and could not recall anything of significance connected with the incident. The same applied to storekeepers and others.

"Nothing strange about it, though," said Deputy Hawkins. "They come and they go, dozens every day, from all over. A bunch operating from the Big Bend country maybe, or even from Mexico. I think I've seen that skinny one somewhere but I ain't sure. Well, it doesn't matter anyhow, the important thing is that they got their comeuppance, the thievin' buzzards! Slade, you ought to be a peace officer, you'd make a dang good one. You've done more to clean up this section since you've been here than the whole sheriff's office."

Eighteen

Mawson, Releford and the Bradded R hands, even the wounded cowboys who had been patched up by the doctor, were jubilant over the outcome of the affair and proceeded to celebrate fittingly in the various saloons, but Walt Slade was in a black mood. To all appearances he had just about cleaned up the rank and file of the outlaw bunch, but the head of the snake was still very much alive, and he knew well that that kind of a "head" would quickly grow a new body.

"Well, I've one more card to play," he told Tom Mawson as they rode home in the light of dawn. "It's up to you and Bob to get busy with your well drilling. The way I see it, everything depends on Ballard and Richardson not knowing that we know what they know, which sounds a bit complicated, but I guess you get what I mean."

"Reckon I do," Mawson agreed. "If they haven't tumbled to the fact that we know they know there's oil under my property they'll go ahead and try to pull something instead of pulling out."

"That's right," Slade nodded. "If they realize that we know all the angles and suspect Ballard is something other than just a saloonkeeper, I'm afraid they will pull out and get completely in the clear. In fact, all they'd need to do is sit tight, for I still haven't a dang thing on them no matter what I think. Well, we'll start things moving and see how it works out. Anyhow, I'm convinced you and Bob will hit the jackpot and that's something."

The project got underway, with Bill Ayers, the pessimistic but highly efficient head driller in charge. Machinery and supplies were purchased and moved onto Mawson's middle pasture several miles north of the creek.

"And this is the craziest one yet," Ayers declared. "Now I know Kent has gone loco."

"That's what you said down on the mesa," Quales the rigger reminded him.

"Uh-huh, but this is worse," Ayers replied. "Who the devil ever heard of oil running uphill! And that's what it would have to do to get here. It's a shame to waste a nice new rotary bit on a dry hole."

He patted the shining metal affectionately. "This thing cost puhlenty, but she'll sure cut through a damn sight faster than an old churn," he added. "Oh, well, we're getting paid for it and we have to work at something."

The rotary did work fast and the bore deepened steadily. The eight-hundred-foot level was reached with the drill thudding on rock after a significant belt of sand. Even Ayers became cautiously optimistic. An old hand at the game, he had noted encouraging signs.

But aside from the steady boring of the drill deeper and deeper in the earth nothing happened. Old Tom began to grow doubtful that anything would.

"I've a notion the sidewinders have caught on and give up," Mawson said. "Everything's been almighty quiet in the section of late. Nothing off-colored happened since they made the try for Tol Releford's money."

"Not particularly surprising for two reasons," Slade pointed out. "In the first place it would take Ballard a little time to get another bunch together. Secondly, he wouldn't want to stir up the section right now. People occupied with their own affairs quickly forget what's taken place and as a result drop their guard. And an experienced oilman like Richardson can figure mighty close just how much money you're spending day by day; and you let it be known how much you were prepared to invest before

215

abandoning the project. They'll want to be sure you're close to scraping the bottom of the barrel before they do anything. They can also figure fairly close just how long it is safe to wait. Admitting that there is an oil pool beneath your land, they can estimate pretty accurately how deep the bore should be before there is likelihood of a strike. Incidentally, I think we're getting mighty close to the required depth. We're hammering rock right now and my guess is that it's the cap-rock over the reservoir. They'll guess that, too, and if they're going to make a move, they'll make it soon. A few well placed sticks of dynamite would smash the bit and the derrick, warp the casing and cave in the well. And it would take a lot of time and money to straighten out such a mess, the money they believe you have no intention of spending. I think they'll make their move any night now."

"Maybe you're right," Mawson conceded, "but I sure wish you'd let me and some of the boys string along with you. I hate to think of you out there alone in the dark every night."

"It's my chore and it's up to me to handle it alone," Slade replied. "Besides, they may be keeping a pretty close watch on us and any undue activity might tip them off."

The following afternoon, when Slade arrived at the scene of the drilling after a few hours' sleep, Ayers approached him.

"If we're going to strike anything," the driller said with his usual pessimistic emphasis, "I've a notion we're mighty close. There's a funny hollow sound been coming up the bore for the last couple of hours. Kent tells me you don't want the well to come in just yet, if it's going to come in."

Slade walked to the well and listened to the muffled thudding of the drill. "I've a notion you're right," he said. "Tell you what, shorten the suspending rope and let the derrick jig with the bit hanging against the casing."

"Okay," agreed the mystified driller. As he moved away to make the necessary adjustment, Slade heard him mutter, "Now I know everybody's loco but me, and I ain't a bit sure about myself."

Night descended with an almost full moon due in a couple of hours. Objects on the prairie were shadowy and unreal. The tall derrick stood ghost-like, a nebulous tracery against the starry sky.

In a thicket less than a score of yards from the bore, Walt Slade lounged comfortably near where his horse was tethered, watching and waiting, as he had done for several nights. Now and then he lighted a cigarette, carefully shielding the faint flicker of the match in his cupped palms. He knew nobody could approach the well without him hearing and seeing them, but he took no chances.

The moon rose, climbing slowly above the eastern hills, the shadows became blockier, objects clearly visible. Midnight came and went, and still the ranger watched and waited. Abruptly he stiffened to attention.

First it was but a whisper of sound coming from the south. It loudened to a pattering, loudened still more to a slow beat of horses' irons on the thick grass. From behind a grove some hundreds of yards to the south appeared a moving clump that quickly materialized to three horsemen riding toward the well.

Slade's eyes narrowed. He had expected only one man, possibly two. Well, he'd have to make the best of it against uncomfortably heavy odds; but the element of surprise would be in his favor.

The riders approached purposefully. A few minutes more and Slade recognized Wade Ballard, Blaine Richardson and Nate Persinger. They drew rein close to the derrick. Richardson and Persinger dismounted. Ballard remained seated on his tall sorrel horse.

Slade noted that Richardson carried something. The next second he saw that what the oilman packed was a bundle of dynamite sticks wrapped together and capped and fused. The pair approached the derrick.

Slade waited a moment longer, until they were beside the bore, so there could be no misinterpretation of their purpose. He drew his guns and stepped from concealment, the star of the rangers gleaming on his broad breast. His voice rang out, shattering the stillness, "Elevate! You're covered! In the name of the State of Texas —"

Wade Ballard opened the ball. He drew from a shoulder holster with unbelievable speed even as Slade lunged to the left. A lock of black hair leaped from the side of the ranger's head; he reeled from the shock of the grazing slug. Wade Ballard whipped his horse around and fled south. Slade couldn't do anything about it; he had his hands full with Richardson and Persinger. A bullet burned its way along his ribs. Another slashed a furrow in his arm. Through the blaze of his Colts he saw Persinger go down to lie without sound or motion. Richardson, partly shielded by a corner of the derrick, was yelling curses as he fired with one hand and brandished the bundle of dynamite with the other. Slade's hat turned sideways on his head. Another slug ripped his shirt sleeve. Steadying himself he took deliberate aim at the oilman and pulled trigger. He saw blood pour down Richardson's face as he plunged forward.

Slade uttered a bitter curse. Richardson's dead hand had done what it hadn't accomplished in life; the bundle of dynamite had dropped squarely down the bore. Slade tensed for the explosion as he raced to where Shadow stood saddled and bridled.

It came as he forked the black, a muffled boom far below. But as he flashed past the derrick his heart leaped exultantly. From the depths of the earth sounded a deep-toned rumbling that rose quickly to a crashing roar. Looking back over his shoulder he saw the derrick fly to a thousand pieces while up and up and up soared a hissing black column that caught the moonlight in prismatic glitters.

"She's in!" he shouted to Shadow. "The dynamite busted the cap-rock and she's in! That's a *gusher!* Spindletop never beat this!"

Turning his back on the thundering well he gave his whole attention to riding, for in Ballard's tall sorrel Shadow had for once very nearly met his match. The yellow horse was almost if not quite as fast as the black.

"But I'm betting he hasn't got your staying qualities, feller," Slade told Shadow. "Sift sand, jughead, that sidewinder is making for Mexico, but we'll get him!"

Far ahead he could see the fugitive, veering westward toward the Chihuahua Trail. A few minutes later, Shadow's irons rang loudly on the hard surface of the track. Ballard was still far ahead, low in the saddle, urging his mount to greater speed.

The lights of Weirton came into view. Shadow foamed through the waters of the creek and went racing up the slope. They topped it and Slade saw that Ballard had not turned aside. He was still riding due south across the mesa.

"I'm afraid he's gaining on us a bit," Slade muttered. "His cayuse is packing a lot lighter load."

The glow of Weirton was left behind. The miles flowed past. In the far distance was what looked like the leaping-off place of the edge of the world; it was where the trail left the mesa and plunged steeply downward to the desert hundreds of feet below.

The east was graying and in the strengthening light of dawn Slade saw Ballard and his speeding horse vanish abruptly as they went over the mesa lip. A few minutes and he, too, was at the crest of the sag. Again he sighted Ballard, nearing the bottom of the slope. And now the yellow horse appeared to be straining a bit, and Slade believed he had gained a little on the fugitive.

"We'll get him," he told Shadow as they went down the sag. But he quickly noted something that gave him no little concern. A wind had risen with the dawn and was steadily strengthening. The surface of the desert was growing misty, which meant that the sands were moving. Let the wind gain in power and soon they would be flying in blinding clouds, and a bad wind storm on the desert was no light thing to reckon with. Slade knew he would be taking a chance if he continued to follow Ballard across the arid wastes; but when he reached the bottom of the sag he sent Shadow forward, urging him to greater speed. The distance between him and his quarry was undoubtedly lessening, but slowly, and already things were becoming a bit blurred. A sudden burst of wind sent clouds of dust flying to all but obscure Ballard's form.

"Trail, Shadow, trail!" he urged. "We've got to catch up with him before the storm really breaks!"

Shadow responded with a gallant burst of speed that quickly halved the distance between him and the sorrel; but now they were feeling the full force of the storm. The air was growing unbearably hot, the flying particles of sand stung Slade's skin like flakes of fire, and he knew this was nothing to what was to come. A warning monitor in his brain told him to give up the chase rather than risk the deadly peril that lay before him. Not so very long before he had nearly lost his life in the Tucumcari Desert in the Panhandle, and the northern desert was mild to this blazing inferno he faced, but he grimly refused to listen and urged the black on.

Ballard's sorrel had given his best; but now he was failing. Despite the swirling clouds of sand, Slade could still make out the form of his quarry. Now they were well out on the desert and exposed to the increasing fury of the wind, heat and flying sand. The air was filled with flickering yellow shadows through which the sun shone like a blood-red orange. Overhead the wind roared with a hollow, tearing sound. The sand particles hissed and whispered. Even bits of gravel were raised from the ground and sent flying through the air like shot.

Slade knew they were off the trail, or what had been a trail. His mouth was growing leathery, his tongue was swelling, his lips cracking. But still the tall sorrel staggered on with Shadow shambling after him, closing the distance stride by stride.

They were miles out in the inferno of dust and heat when the climax came. Slade, peering through the shrouding dust, saw Ballard pull his horse to a halt and swing him around. A spurt of flame pierced the shadows, the bullet zipped past Slade's face. He jerked his right-hand gun and answered the other shot for shot.

There was no chance to take aim. One instant the target stood out in bold relief, the next it was obscured by the swirling dust clouds. The two forms were weird, blurred shadows amid the shadows, blasting death at one another through the yellow murk.

Slade heard the hammer click on an empty shell. He pulled his left-hand gun and fired again and again. This time he counted the shots; there would be no chance to reload. Ballard was bearing down on him, looming gigantic in the yellow gloom.

Four — five — Slade held his breath and squeezed the trigger just as the world around him exploded in flame and roaring sound. He reeled in the saddle and fell sideways, clutching at the horn for support. His despairing grip on the leather checked his descent and he slid to the ground, still grasping the pommel sagging against the horse's barrel, blood streaming down the left side of his face. Some corner of his brain still alive and active forbade his stiffening fingers to loosen their grip on the saddle horn; otherwise he would have died, buried and smothered by the falling sand.

Slade never quite lost consciousness. Numb, dazed, his whole left side seemingly paralyzed by the terrific blow of the creasing bullet, he clung tenaciously to the pommel, leaning against his shivering horse while the hot sand drifted down in clouds.

NINETEEN

How long he stood there, Walt Slade never knew; but when his senses began functioning something like normal, his hat brim was sagging with the weight of the accumulated sand. The numbed fingers of his left hand still gripped his empty gun. He holstered it and with trembling fingers traced a ragged furrow just above his left temple, from which blood still oozed sluggishly. He shook some of the sand from his hat and glanced about dazedly. Nearby was something vague and distorted in the shadows, which he finally recognized as Ballard's sorrel horse. But all around him save for the moan and roar of the wind and the whispering of the sands was a vast silence.

Deciding he could stand without support he released his hold on the saddle horn and after a moment of uncertain weaving stumbled forward, reeling but keeping his feet till he fell over some object. Doggedly he got to his hands and knees and saw what had tripped him was the body of a man already partially mounded over. He scraped away some of the sand and peered into Wade Ballard's dead face. In death it looked strangely peaceful, the shadow of his perpetual smile still on his lips. Slade experienced a feeling of regret that a man of such ability had ridden a crooked trail to die in the lonely wasteland. He wondered dully if he could pack the body to town and give it a decent burial, but realized it was impossible; a deadly nausea was sweeping over him, his head was pounding, his eyes refusing to focus properly. He struggled to his feet and stumbled to where his horse stood. After several unsuccessful tries he managed to climb into the saddle. He turned and called to Ballard's horse, his voice a mere rasping croak. The exhausted animal followed, shambling after Shadow.

The details of that frightful ride remained forever blurred and unreal to Walt Slade. At times he knew he was muttering and gabbling with delirium. Twice he started to slide from the saddle and only saved himself by a frantic clutch at the horn. Finally he leaned forward onto the horse's neck and twined his fingers into the coarse hair of its mane.

He was aroused from the deadly apathy by the clash of Shadow's irons on stone. He raised his head and saw a huge dark mass looming before him. It was the wall of the mesa rising from the desert floor. And here the air was a bit clearer, the heat not quite so intense. His mind cleared somewhat. Which way should he turn to reach the trail and the only way to the crest? After a moment of deliberation, his plainsman's instinct told him to turn to the left. Hugging the jagged wall, he sent the tired horse forward, the sorrel lurching along behind. After what seemed an eternity he saw the gray ribbon of the trail winding up the slope. A few more minutes and they were in clear air and Slade revived quickly. He knew that a little stream meandered across the mesa not far from its lip, and made for it. The horses, scenting the water, quickened their pace to a shambling trot. They reached the creek bank and thrust their noses into the water. Slade tumbled from the saddle and drank all he dared. He forced the animals away from the stream, removed the bits and allowed them to graze.

After a while he permitted them more water and drank a little more himself. Then he bandaged his wounded head and his bullet-cut arm.

"Okay, fellers," he told the horses, "let's head for where we can get some real chuck."

Mounting Shadow he rode to Weirton and a livery stable where with the help of a keeper he gave both animals a good rubdown.

"Let them have some oats and water with a little whiskey in it," he directed. "I'll be back for mine after a while."

"Okay, Ranger," the keeper answered, gazing curiously at the star on Slade's breast. "Hardly anybody left in town right now; they're all up at the oil strike on Tom Mawson's land. Understand there's a gusher what is a gusher up there."

Feeling uncommonly hungry, Slade repaired to the Black Gold, which he found practically deserted, and ordered a meal. He was eating when old Tom Mawson came hurrying in, his face anxious. He raised a shout of relief when he spied Slade.

"Been looking for you all over," he said. "I figured maybe you'd be down this way. What the devil happened?"

Slade told him, briefly, for he was very tired and didn't feel much like talking. Old

Tom listened, shaking his head and tugging his mustache.

"The noise the well made coming in woke everybody up," he said. "We hustled down there and found the bodies of Richardson and Persinger. They were sort of busted up by stuff that fell on them but we saw the bullet holes and knew you must have had a showdown with them. All the oilmen are up there trying to cap the well. I never heard such cussing. The boys and everybody else who can get hold of a pick or a shovel are building a reservoir to hold the oil that's spilling all over the place. She's sure a whizzer. Bob Kent says he never saw anything like it. Looks like you were right on all counts."

"I reckon," Slade smiled wearily. "Now I'm heading for the ranchhouse and bed. I feel as if I'd been drug through a knothole and hung on a barbed wire fence to dry."

On the way home they paused at the spouting well, where the blaspheming riggers were toiling furiously to anchor the cap valve while a swarm of willing workers labored to deepen and widen and embank the reservoir that received the overflow.

"We'll have her under control before dark," said oil-smeared Bill Ayers. "She's a lulu just as I always said she'd be when she came in." Quales grinned and winked at Slade.

"And now, son, I suppose you'll be pulling out," remarked old Tom as they rode away. "You sure did a wonderful chore down here. Everybody was out gunning for everybody else and trouble in every direction. Now everybody's working together and plumb peaceful. Wade Ballard's got himself a nice cozy resting place under the sand and Richardson and Persinger will be planted tomorrow. Yes, a mighty good chore. I heard today the railroad has already started building south and Weirton Valley and everybody aims to be happy and prosperous. We'll sure hate to see you go. But we won't say goodbye, we'll just say *hasta luego,* like the Mexicans do."

"Yes," Slade nodded, "till we meet again!"

"What about the drillers and riggers who worked for Richardson?" Mawson asked.

"I figure they were just hired hands and didn't take a really active part in the trouble," Slade replied. "Put them to work and forget about them."

"Yep, that's a good notion," agreed old Tom. "That's just what I'll do."

Two days later Walt Slade rode away from the Walking M. "I've got to get back to the post and report to Captain McNelty," he told Mary. "The chances are he'll have another little chore lined up for me by the time I get there."

On the rimrock he pulled Shadow to a halt and for some moments sat gazing back toward where Weirton huddled beneath its smoke cloud. All around the town stretched the emerald and amethyst billows of the rangeland. In its beauty Walt Slade envisioned a promise of peace, prosperity and content.

El Halcon smiled and turned away. Along the crest of the hills he rode, his eyes dream-filled, to where duty, danger and new adventure waited.

We hope you have enjoyed this Large Print book. Other Thorndike, Wheeler, and Chivers Press Large Print books are available at your library or directly from the publishers.

For information about current and upcoming titles, please call or write, without obligation, to:

Publisher
Thorndike Press
295 Kennedy Memorial Drive
Waterville, ME 04901
Tel. (800) 223-1244

or visit our Web site at:

www.gale.com/thorndike
www.gale.com/wheeler

OR

Chivers Large Print
published by BBC Audiobooks Ltd
St James House, The Square
Lower Bristol Road
Bath BA2 3SB
England
Tel. +44(0) 800 136919
email: bbcaudiobooks@bbc.co.uk
www.bbcaudiobooks.co.uk

All our Large Print titles are designed for easy reading, and all our books are made to last.